LIFE'S A
B*TCH

GEORGE ONSTOT

ISBN-13: 978-0-9919396-1-9
ISBN-10: 0991939611

ALSO BY GEORGE ONSTOT

PUBLISHED BY

THE GOOD WORD

PART ONE

ONE

Sheri Rawson told everybody that I loved football more than I loved her. I hadn't said any such thing. I hadn't thought it, either, and I wasn't dumb enough to say such a thing, either. She started her "he loves *it* more than he loves *me*" shit while I was still Red Crossley playing for the Bayporte Invaders of the National Football League. A legend in my own mind, the guy they expected to get suited up every Sunday and find some way to *win*. My stats were good my enthusiasm constant. As long as I remained healthy and productive, the Invaders were a viable contender to enter the postseason. Then Sheri started in with, "Red loves Tia Gomez more than he loves me." Excuse me? Sheri was my wife, not Tia. Damn women. I'll never figure them out, and I can't keep them happy for long.

As you probably know, a concussion reduced my NFL career to absolute zero. Suddenly, I had to suit up each Sunday just to sit on the bench. Our coach thought I could boost morale just by sitting there and cheering on the team..

During one game, a future Hall of Famer named Painless O'Neal took me down with a tackle that made me forget my own name.

Here is what our general manager probably said in his office: "I sure wish we had Red Crossley on Sunday. But he's got those concussions, you see. He would give us everything he's got, but he doesn't have very much left to give. He's one of the best Invaders we've ever had, when he could play. Maybe with rehab, we'll get him up to eighty percent, but eighty isn't a hundred, and we need a hundred percent of Red Crossley to win. I don't care about the global financial crisis. The only thing I care about right now is Red's well-being."

The game that became the beginning of the end for me happened, as these things so often do, on our opening day last season. Painless, whose contract with the Toronto Stars had expired, huddled with his agent and they both decided that the best thing would be to sell Painless' services to the highest bidder, which turned out to be the New York Giants. I had worked out during the off-season and looked forward to another season with the Invaders.

More power to ya, my admirers said. I had been born and raised in Bayporte and attended my city's huge Northup University. A kid who scarcely knew the difference between aerobics and disrobics.

So when I got hurt, it seemed to me—and many others—that my medical problems had more global significance than the War on Terrorism. *The New York Times* considered it a big deal, too. It ran this sports headline:

RED CROSSLEY HURT; WHAT NOW?

They said other things, too.

That awful game was on national television, so many people saw it as it happened, and millions of others have seen it on YouTube. They ask me about it when I make banquet appearances during the off-season.

A person will say, "Cross, tell us about Painless O'Neal." I'll say something like, "Candyass O'Neal?

What do you want to know about him?"

My concussion that day was merely the first in a series of dreadful events that changed my life and those of my friends. That year would be, for us, the dumbest one of our football lives.

Yessir, that year was mostly chaotic.

My concussion became a very trivial matter.

The game where Painless took me down wasn't played in Kosovo, although it might as well have been. The New York Giants, which had acquired Painless from the Toronto Stars, had moved to New Jersey.

We, the Bayporte Invaders, had almost moved to New Jersey, if one could believe the rumors, because NuWest Sports, the company that owns us, changed owners, and the new owner, Jack Piros, privately assured me that the rumors were bullshit. Those rumors were meant to scare Bayporte football fans into valuing their team more.

"We won't be moving," Jack had said. "But they've built a new stadium in Jersey. I figure the Electric Daisy Carnival will be a yearly tenant, and they'll get Bruce Springsteen to perform there."

I had said to my teammates, "That Jersey rumor? It's all bullshit. They would have to rename us the Manhattan Haters."

Those New Jersey rumors irked me. We had won the Super Bowl at home, which wasn't supposed to happen. They did the lottery to determine the site of the Big Game, and Bayporte ended up becoming the location. That year, we, the Invaders ended up taking on the other Canadian franchise, the Toronto Stars.

Wilbert "Flash" Gortton and I made some big plays that day, too.

But at NuWest Sports in downtown Bayporte, the suits on the top floor are involved in the nasty business of tax avoidance. They've all read about how New York City took a big old porno theatre in Times Square, renovated it at the taxpayers' expense and gave—not sold, *gave*—it to Disney so they could show kiddie crap to tourists.

For a little while I genuinely feared that those rumors had some substance. NuWest Sports wanted someone to give them a fancy new sports facility that could hold up to 100,000 people and deluxe boxes for the rich folks. If the place looked more like a hotel than a sports facility, so what?

You can believe this: A team owner's greed will determine most of the major decisions he'll make.

"Of course, we're stayin' in Bayporte, but for a dozen reasons, we're back to playing bad football," said my teammate L.T. Briggs, a behemoth tackle. "They're just laughin' at us, and we probably deserve it."

L.T. felt much angrier over our poor performance than he did about the rumors of our relocation to New Jersey. L.T., a football maniac, hated even the thought of losing a game. On the field, he would grunt and scream like a zoo beast, and he'd come off the field with his face scratched and bloody. He always gave a hundred and ten percent, an expression coaches never used but sportscasters always loved.

L.T. distinguished himself in another way: He'd gone out to play without ever sticking a needle into his ass beforehand.

When a sportswriter asked him how he managed

to get "pumped up for action," L.T. replied, "Oh, Coach just comes by and says, 'It's football time, ladies.'"

L.T., after a dozen seasons with the Invaders, retired, or was cut, and accepted a coaching position at Rainier College near Seattle. I met them at the airport to say goodbye. His wife Darla, a corn-fed Midwestern cheerleader, gave me a hug and a smile. "We're gonna do fine in Seattle," she said, "because there won't be many Chinks or Pakis around."

L.T. pumped my hand. "This is just what I want at this stage of my life: To help today's boys become tomorrow's football studs."

I wondered how, in these politically correct times, Rainier's black players would react to being called niggers, which L.T. would do whenever they failed to catch a pass or make a tackle. L.T. had been around black people all of his life; his roommate at Clemson, Pol Pott, had played alongside him for the Invaders. A black remained a black till he did something wrong, and then he became a nigger, just as a white boy who fucked up became a Polack, mick, fairy or kike.

We all felt astonished when L.T. went to Seattle and made Rainier College's team one of the most successful in the Pacific Northwest. Half of his players were black, and I guess they put up with him. I could hear him saying to his running back, "Leroy, if you puke up that football one more time, I'm gonna put my boot up your barbecue-lovin' backside!"

I think Woody Hayes would have liked L.T.'s coaching style, and I admired his results.

"I like to scare 'em," L.T. told me. "Fear is a great motivator. They need to put the fear back into football, Cross. Today they're afraid to touch the quarterback or make a late hit. Today's football is nothing but chickenshit, and I'm tryin' to change all that. My boys, if they don't put points on the board or force the other team to punt, what do I do? I take away their cars, their money, their pussy, their weed. Sometimes I even put them in jail. The police and I have ourselves a little agreement about that."

L.T. then did something I found shocking: He returned to Bayporte as the new head coach of the Northup Kodiaks. My alma mater. Flash's and Sheri's, too.

The big man scored a five-year contract with the U. They brought him aboard to make the football team a winner again, because they wanted Northup to be known for something other than engineering and agricultural science.

L.T. arrived at his new job full of piss and swagger. He said to all of those who cared to listen—and many did, including me—"We gonna wake this big bear up. Them Kodiaks been hibernatin' too damn long."

The new coach had an old problem: He couldn't recruit the best players. The elite athletes graduating from high schools in Great Elizabeth, and elsewhere in Canada, rarely considered becoming Kodiaks. Instead, they went to the University of Toronto, the University of British Columbia or, if they were really outstanding, the American colleges would offer them athletic scholarships.

"I just don't get it, Red," L.T. said to me on the phone. "You would think these would be grateful to be in college, playin' football, but once you start yellin' at them on the practice field, they get an attitude and say, 'Don't speak to *me* like that!' How the fuck am I supposed to speak to them? Should I say, 'Pretty please with sugar on top'?"

He'd learned, in a couple of years, far more than he ever wanted to know about coaching at a big-time school. The Kodiaks lost three times as many games as they won. L.T. stood on the sidelines horrified as his boys stumbled through one game after another, but whenever one of us asked him for an explanation, he said, "This losin' stuff won't last forever. We're just gonna keep at it till we get our act together."

I believe the moment when L.T. began to overcome his struggle was the evening when he, half drunk, called me and said, "Red, tell you what: You and Flash Gortton need to help me get that spade who's down in Louisiana."

Flash Gortton, my greatest friend, liked to pretend that football was a hobby he could walk away from at any time. His motto, often repeated, was, "Nothing matters and what if it did?"

Flash, Sheri and I went back as far as elementary school. We were fortunate enough, the three of us, to stay chummy throughout childhood, and Sheri even enrolled at Northup with us to keep our little threesome intact. After graduation, I rejoiced at the Invaders' interest in Flash and me. We were as close as two men could be without having sex.

Flash and I ended up screwing some of the same women, too, including Sheri Rawson, who later became my missus.

I won't talk just yet about my pal's virility, which could have made John C. Holmes envious. Let me just say that I had never met anyone, and probably never will encounter anyone, who could catch footballs as consistently and effortlessly as Flash did.

As a pass receiver, Flash would sprint past his opponents like a spy sneaking through enemy lines. Springing into the air like a hang-glider, he would return to earth with the ball on his fingertips, then he'd dash past the defensive players as if they were standing there merely to admire him.

One Sunday, after Flash had made four spectacular touchdown catches against the Baltimore Ravens, I said to him, "Dammit, Flash, you're more precious than oil!"

"Just another day at the office, Red," Flash replied.

His nonchalance about the seriousness of life almost got me punched out during a high school game in Bayporte one evening.

We attended Oliver Johnson Secondary School, neither the best nor the worst in our city, but just about the biggest.

The boys at "O.J." wore Levi's jeans and jackets, T-shirts silkscreened with beer ads, and we wore our hair like Billie Jean King.

That evening, we played the other team on their turf. The boys at that school shaved their heads and vandalized cars in other neighborhoods.

Throughout the game, a notorious skinhead named Gerdi Weber kept facemasking and kicking Flash when the referee wasn't looking. I assumed Weber did those things because Flash was a great football player and, as the girls would say, "a hottie." We knew Gerdi as someone who misspelled the naughty words he spray-painted on buildings and threatened the lives of teachers who gave him failing grades. His vocabulary consisted mainly of "Fuck off, goof" and "You're dead after school."

In the fourth quarter, Flash called a timeout and confronted Gerdi. Flash, helmet in hand, walked over to Gerdi and smiled like an ancient holy man.

But after looking humble and peaceful for a moment or two, Flash said, "Listen here, Gerdi. If you don't stop picking on me, Cross is going to kick your balls up through the roof of your mouth, and you won't be able to fuck your sister anymore."

Gerdi hauled off with a roundhouse swing that missed Flash, who ducked with the deftness of a Hollywood stuntman. But the punch took out a few of the zebra's teeth, and I lost a couple myself in the melee that followed.

Flash, naturally, went untouched throughout the ugliness. In fact, while my opponent and I tried to choke each other unconscious, I stole a peek over at Flash as he chatted up Carrie Pesht, the only O.J. cheerleader who would give us oral pleasure.

One afternoon at O.J., Flash performed an athletic feat so extraordinary that I still think about it sometimes.

The remarkable incident started on the playground during gym class. A bunch of us on the football team goofed off by playing a very informal game of touch-tackle. Our game, and a softball game, happened right next to each other, and nobody could tell where one ended and the other began. Also, we were fairly close to the high-jump area.

Flash caught a pass, then fled his would-be tacklers and presently entered the softball diamond, whereupon he caught a line drive with his free hand, tagged out a baserunner and, once in the end zone, cleared the six-foot-plus high-jump bar.

Afterwards, at Paul's Submarine Sandwich Stop,

Flash won half a dozen free games on the Atari video machine. A few hours later, on our double date in Sheri's father's Lincoln Continental, Flash ravished her into throes of ecstasy, then suavely persuaded Ally Rempel to put out for me as a special favor to *him*.

After that day, I went through life believing that Flash could move mountains if he wanted to.

Football, like most other things, came so easily to Flash that he had some difficulty taking it seriously and having respect for it. The Invaders paid him almost as much as he wanted, so he stayed put for longer than he otherwise might have. But throughout his NFL career, he spoke to me about his other options in life.

"I want to do something meaningful and fulfilling, Red," he told me every other day.

"Don't talk like that," I told him. "Just be here now."

He grinned in spite of himself. *Be Here Now* was one of his favorite books.

"I want," he said, "to become a famous writer."

Flash had suffered from this obsession since our time at Northup, when he went to all the artsy-fartsy foreign movies and watched David Suzuki's nature programs. He also read as many esoteric books as he could find in the Northup library.

Northup wasn't Harvard, and Bayporte wasn't Cambridge, but we did have decent bookstores for eggheads and theatres showing Hollywood trash. Plus, we had girls with tits. Bayporte women are more than adequate most of the time. Even Flash couldn't complain—he'd done as many of 'em as he could.

Flash read books, heavier than slabs of cement, that had been written by nerds and geeks with names I couldn't even begin to pronounce.

"Biggest, thickest fuckin' thing I've ever touched," I said, lifting one of his borrowed tomes. "Damn thing probably just says, 'Life's a bitch and then you die.' I don't like books that say you're fucked."

"Read one," Flash replied. "We'll talk about it."

He soon concluded that his heavy reading had taught him all he needed to learn. "I'm now thinking what a shame it would be if I passed up the chance to share with others what I have come to know," he told me. "Especially since I'm someone people pay attention to. It's time for me to start writing."

"Do you know *how* to write?" I asked him.

"Shit, Red, there's nothing to it. Just sit there and hit the keys."

"Really?"

He shrugged. "Yeah. Then go on the lecture and speaking tour. Go to different cities, stand at the lectern, read a few pages, answer a few questions. Writers are the rock stars of the college set, you see. Every boy wants to know them and every girl wants to blow them."

"I've never been horny for women who wear glasses, read books and go to places where they can listen to the people who write those books. Those kinds of women just don't appeal to me," I said.

"Well, Red, think again. As athletes, we've missed out on a huge amount of literary pussy. If you'd ever troubled yourself to read a novel, you would know what dirty little minds those literary ladies have."

After our Super Bowl victory, Flash remained in football for another season, but I could tell that he'd put himself mainly on autopilot.

We spent countless hours in bars, lounges and other dark, seductive places, holding up our Super Bowl rings and gazing at them as if we were the only people in the world who owned such goodies.

Our rings, gorgeous and golden and chunky, glittered with diamonds. Each ring had a big round onyx in the shape of a football. We loved speaking into those rings like a couple of James Bonds.

"Prepare for getting bombed," one of us would say into his finger as another round of Canadian Comforts over ice arrived.

We might be in one of a dozen bars in Manhattan where they served booze till dawn.

Regardless of our location, one of us at one point would say, "Scuds on deck!"

That meant everyone should be aware of the voluptuous woman who had just walked in.

On some evenings, Sheri would hang out with us. By midnight, she would lean over and speak into someone's ring, "Bored shitless, returning to hotel."

Our Super Bowl team became the laughingstock of the NFL soon after Flash retired to devote himself to the literary life. Quarterback Vernon Braithwaite, defensive lineman Pol Pott and several other star players left the Invaders. Vernon quit so he could try making some bad investments.

Pol Pott, our best offensive lineman, teamed up

with Painless O'Neal of the Toronto Stars and attempted to organize a players' strike that did not materialize. That's why the Stars traded Painless to New York and the Invaders traded Pott to the 49ers.

Pol felt pleased to move to San Francisco. He had gotten sick of Bayporte's nonstop rain and sought the bliss of northern California's fog.

Stu Bobbits, our cornerback, beat his statutory rape charge, but the scandal and its attendant publicity freaked him out. He married his girlfriend as soon as she came of age and they moved to Florida.

"Calling Bobbits a retard," said Flash, "is an insult to retarded people everywhere."

Mickey Ruckerton became a homosexual, or perhaps had always been that way. He outed himself in a magazine interview. The news disturbed everyone but surprised few of us; most of us had long ago surmised which team *he* played for.

Mitch Stemmens, our free safety, didn't know the DEA was after him until the feds burst into his apartment near Seattle and arrested him with fifty pounds of methamphetamine stashed inside his closet. They gave him fifteen years.

Mitch handled it all like a man. He made parole after three years. Guys from around the NFL sent him things they knew he would enjoy—food, clothing, pornographic magazines—because he flatly refused to name any of his connections. Everyone respected him for that. Mitch was no snitch.

These men compromised the core of our team— along with L.T., Flash and me, of course—so when they departed, we knew quite well why the Invaders declined.

In the midst of our free-fall, the team

sought to rebuild our dynasty. The bosses failed abysmally; they hired every bit of flotsam and jetsam the other teams had put on waivers.

One week we brought on board a temperamental millionaire kid who refused to learn our playbook and insisted on bringing his business adviser. Other times, we procured a shit disturber who, cut loose by half a dozen teams, came to us with a nickname like "Attitude" or "Slacker."

I finished every game bloodied and bruised, and it seemed that the harder I tried, the fewer points we scored. Flash had a very astute football mind, so as we sat in a bar I asked him what the Invaders' biggest problems were.

"Red," he said after staring off into space for a few minutes, "I would rather try to describe to Stevie Wonder what the Planet Earth looks like."

Flash worked on his novel during his final football season. He even toyed with the notion of selling his equity in our Bayporte highrise condominium and moving to SoHo, Tribeca or the East Village because he'd read that some of the greatest American and foreign writers had done their best work in those neighborhoods.

"To tell you the truth," he said, "I think that *all* districts in Manhattan are creatively stimulating."

But he decided against moving after Sheri reminded him that Manhattan had an abundance of two things he disliked: vegetarian restaurants and no-smoking areas.

I wondered about Flash as a writer. I dreaded seeing him in a Che Guevara beret, tweed jacket with suede elbow patches or Gucci loafers, but fortunately such changes did not happen.

He did begin to scratch things down on the nearest scrap of paper, and even grew a goatee. But Flash was Hollywood handsome; the face fuzz, like everything else, looked good on him.

His novel was called *Action Man*. Here I must make a confession: I didn't get past the first page. Few people did.

In his first draft, his first paragraph was this:

Let me tell you what I did the day after I committed suicide.

When he showed me the first chapter one evening so that I could see what he was up to. "I didn't know that dead men could do stuff after killing themselves."

"In literature," he explained, "all things are possible."

Flash probably expected such feedback from me, a semiliterate running back who'd made an embarrassing attempt at writing a memoir. I had failed not because my book lacked artistic significance, but because upon completing it I read it over and recognized it for the turd it truly was.

Flash, like Hemingway, rewrote each paragraph dozens of times. Finally, it finally reached the virtual and brick-and-mortar bookstores and sold very well in Okie places. But people everywhere else ignored it. The publisher ordered a first printing of 2,000 copies, which pleased Mairi Silver, Flash's agent.

"Pussy in publishing?" Flash confided. "It's

actually overrated. Maybe Mairi works harder for her most famous clients. I kind of didn't like her at first. She outweighed me and had hairier armpits.

"I'm happy to be published, of course, but the reviews for *Action Man* have been scathing."

The book critic for *The New Yorker* wrote, "The makers of Sominex should worry that *Action Man* will put more people to sleep than their over-the-counter tablets."

The critic, an English professor at Bard College, continued: "The publisher of this novel should be ashamed of itself for sending off this manuscript to be printed and bound. This is just another case of other, worthwhile writers being ignored while some famous, uncouth athlete gets the satisfaction of seeing his hardcover novel on bookstore shelves."

"Oh, is my book for sale out there?" Flash asked. "*I* sure as hell can't find it anywhere."

Mairi Silver got all excited when *The New Yorker* reviewed Flash's novel. "Being panned by *them* is quite a compliment. Without their attention, you're nothing."

"I would rather be nothing," Flash told her.

The critic said more:

In *Action Man,* rookie novelist Wilbert "Flash" Gortton, a retired football star, throws open his door and takes his reader for a ride. Trouble is, he has no specific destination in mind. How long should his reader sit there and cruise along with him to nowhere special? Gortton cannot seem to answer this question.

"What happened? Why did they piss all over my

book?" Flash asked Mairi Silver.

"You failed to challenge yourself," she said. "You played it safe."

"I didn't challenge myself? Shit, I learned to use Word for Mac, didn't I?" Then, "It's no fun writing fiction if my novel isn't selling. I'm going to start writing non-fiction."

He started writing *What to Do When Life's a B*tch*, a book whose title is self-explanatory. He also did pieces for men's and general-interest magazines. They wanted him to drop plenty of names, which he did. Lots of people wanted to know that Michael Jackson was even weirder than they thought, or that Sammy Davis, Jr. had once given a blow job to Linda Lovelace's husband.

Flash's foray into journalism added much confusion to our lives following my collision with Painless O'Neal on the football field.

. . .

I want to tell you about that play.

We had made it to New York's five-yard line in the third quarter. We trailed by two touchdowns and needed to get into the end zone, if only to boost our morale. Soon we reached fourth down, and I felt sure we would have a pass play, so one can imagine my astonishment when our quarterback called for something else.

He called my number! He wanted me to do a sweep, which had worked well when Pol Pott, our gargantuan lineman, blocked for me. We used that play in the closing seconds of the Super Bowl when we beat the Toronto Stars, that all-Canadian Super Bowl, the only Super Bowl ever worth talking about.

But this time was different, of course.

Pol Pott at that moment was probably greeting guests at Pol's, his restaurant in San Francisco. His replacement, Pete Alverson, blocked for me by curling up and covering his junk as soon as our center snapped the ball.

Also, Painless O'Neal, the scariest son of a bitch on this or any other football field, played on the defensive line now, which made things very different for me. On that wonderful Super Bowl Sunday when I made the winning touchdown, Painless had played cornerback, which made it much easier for me to get away from him.

Every Stars fan would be quick to remind the world that Painless had injured his ankle during the final minutes of that unforgettable Super Bowl. He stood on the sideline, helmet-less and scowling, as I half-jumped into the end zone for the game-winning score.

True Stars fans, after we beat their team in the Big One on our own turf, burned some of downtown Bayporte and looted our best stores.

Well, on this afternoon in New York, Painless the defensive lineman had an extra edge I hadn't anticipated: He had gobbled a bunch of uppers earlier on the sideline when he thought no Invader was watching.

Painless and I had admired each other for years. On the field we had tackled and grabbed at each other like gay porn stars. This afternoon, I knew we would be foolish to keep running the ball at him when he was all wired nice and tight on pills, his eyes darting everywhere, his tongue constantly moving over his huge lips.

Painless looked so terrifying that I resolved to go

nowhere near him and balked when Davy Carpenter called my number in the huddle.

"Fuck!" I said to him. "You want to send me straight at *Painless*?"

"We'll surprise them," he said.

I shook my head. "We won't be surprising anyone. They'll be expecting it."

"Just do it, Red," Carpenter said. "Scoot right by his black ass and win this damn thing."

"Painless is high as a motherfucker right now," I said. "Throw a pass into the end zone. We'll win it that way."

"Can't throw. My hand's too tired."

"Are you *trying* to lose this game?"

Like an idiot, I shut my mouth and took the handoff from Carpenter. I did my thing the usual way—nothing fancy, neither too fast nor too slow—and tried not to make contact with Painless O'Neal.

For a moment or two, I thought I would get away with it.

I don't think he actually hit me so much as he, with little effort, held me in the in the air as I tried to jump past him. I crumpled to the ground and don't remember much more.

I woke up with an excruciating headache.

"Ohhhh," I said at my teammates and trainer.

"Need a stretcher, Red? Can you hear me?" asked our trainer.

"Ummmmm," I said.

After an hour. or maybe just a couple of minutes, our trainer asked me again if I needed a stretcher or some help getting off the field, and I rose of my own volition.

As our trainer and a couple of other guys walked

me off the field to a smattering of applause, I took a deep breath and thought: I've finally done it. I've gotten so banged up in the head that they'll I'll never let me play again.

Before we entered the tunnel, I saw an obese woman in Giants apparel. Her jowls and massive breasts jiggled as she screamed at me while we walked away.

"Crossley, you loser! Painless finally got to you, huh? Bet it hurts! Go back to Canada and rot! You hear me?"

In the tunnel, one of the trainers looked at me and said, "Red, how'd you like to live with that fat broad and listen to her all the time?"

"Wouldn't be a problem. Just stick a couple of Twinkies into her mouth and shut the bitch up."

In the dressing room, our physician, Dr. Joshua Drori, gave me an MRI.

"I can't say I'm surprised to see you with another concussion," he told me, "but this one's pretty bad. I don't think that, in good conscience, I can sign off for you to play football again. Head injuries are bad news."

I knew enough about such injuries—this one and the others I'd had—to expect that Doc Drori would tell me to go to Plan B, and if I didn't already have one, to get one.

"This," I said to the doctor, "is the end of my football career. Is that what you're telling me?"

"Determination, Red, is a good thing," he said. "Determination always helps in the recovery process. We in the doctor business always like to see patients show determination."

"I'm going to play again," I said.

Dr. Joshua Drori looked down at me and smiled. "Negative. I'm going to put you in hospital for a few days to run some tests when we get back to Bayporte."

"I want a private room with a good view in a private hospital with a TV that has three hundred channels."

...

My guests in the hospital that evening were Jack Piros, the high-technology entrepreneur and new owner of the Bayporte Invaders, his wife Kathleen, and Eddie Lowelling, our aging coach.

"How they hanging, big boy?" Jack asked, his eyes scanning the room as if he were a *Michelin Guide* critic checking out a new restaurant. "Look, I know that right now things seem hopeless for you. But guess what? All hope is *not* lost! That's right! We'll take you to the best hospitals and get the best specialists to see you! Isn't that terrific?"

Kathleen Piros took s seat and read through a magazine. I sat up and winced with pain. Eddie Lowelling looked down at me as if his entire offensive attack had been destroyed, which was essentially the case.

"That nigger Painless?" Eddie said. "It's all his fault. Wait till we play him again."

Jack Piros couldn't stand still. "I talked to the media about Red Crossley. Know what I said? I told them that Red will be back next year. You'll be back and we'll be back in the Super Bowl! Say, Red, is everything here adequate? Is the food edible? If not, just say so and I'll get you Chinese or whatever else you'd like."

Jack Piros, a fidgety billionaire who always wore

Izod shirts and Levi's, had made his fortune as the founder of BrainsCan, a company manufacturing teensy computers that surgeons implanted into the skulls of paralyzed stroke victims. His devices, designed to send messages from the brain to wake up the paralyzed areas, had worked as often as not, and Jack insisted that the only thing preventing his little machines from curing *all* stroke victims was time— that and research. He assured the world he and his team of brainiacs could create itsy-bitsy computers that would be even more sophisticated.

"Television!" Jack Piros exclaimed, snapping his fingers as he stood over my hospital bed. "You'll go on the air once you're mobile again. You'll do color commentary on network-televised NFL games. Starting right now, you have an entire year to be a couch potato and watch the boob tube. Sound OK?

"I'm sure ABC, NBC, CBS and Fox would love to get your services. There might be a bidding war and the only winner would be Red Crossley."

I looked up at him. "You mean it?"

"Does the Pope speak Catholic?"

I guffawed.

"You think you've made good money as an Invader?" he asked. "TV is God's way of allowing certain people to make easy money. Al Michaels, Bob Costas, Tim McCarver, John Madden, Joe Buck? Do you have any idea of what kind of megabucks those guys pull down?"

Jack pumped his hips. "See what I'm doing? I'm fucking, which is what you'll do to the network when it comes time to talk money. Go get 'em!"

I shook my head. "I wouldn't be any good on TV. I'm Canadian. I have a funny accent. They would laugh at me in the States."

Jack frowned. "Are you kidding me? Have you ever listened to Tim McCarver? He's a good ole boy from the South and no one gives a shit about his country bumpkin twang. All you would have to do on TV is watch the fuckin' game and say what you think after each play, which is pretty much what you've been doing all your life."

Eddie Lowelling wiped a tear from his eye. "Guess it's time to go." He took a long look at me. "Third World. That's where Painless and those others come from. Should never have brought them over as slaves."

Kathleen Piros tried to succor me by looking around my room and saying, "This isn't much, is it? At least they could have put you in something a bit more attractive."

A former model, bone-thin Kathleen wore her brown hair cropped close to the skull, like a Castro Street homosexual. Her gaunt face consisted mostly of eyes and cheekbones. I felt sure she wished my hospital room was a Versace boutique where she could whip out her American Express black card and pick up a few nice things.

"Has Sheri had any work done yet?" She meant cosmetic surgery.

"Nothing that she's told me about. But she does things without telling me. Right now, she's in California, doing a pilot for one of the networks."

"She's getting up there," Kathleen said.

"Aren't we all?" I retorted.

She pursed her lips and nodded, as if I'd just told her that her favorite designer had died.

They left presently, and I got a call from Painless

O'Neal. L.T. Briggs, former teammates like Pol Pott and Vernon Braithwaite. A few guys from the Bayporte sports media.

They all said: Stay strong and keep it real.

Flash Gortton called me from somewhere. He was on a promotional tour for the paperback release of *What to Do When Life's a B*tch*. His book had been a nonfiction chart-topper for much of the previous year.

Mairi Silver, Flash's agent, had gotten another publishing house to release the book in softcover because Silver had a friend at Blandford Publishing who agreed that Flash's book was a good fit for readers who were sick of books dealing with diets, exercise and financial frugality.

Flash's book sold nearly half a million copies, although it hardly challenged *Work a Little, Earn a Lot*, the top title on all the major bestseller lists. Nevertheless, his book's sales had made Flash Gortton a moderately respected writer. As such, he had to make at least one radio and TV appearance in practically every decent-sized city in North America *plus* screw Mairi Silver and her girlfriend over at Blandford Publishing.

"Red," he said, "I used to think that making photocopies and stuffing envelopes were the hardest parts of being a writer. But I've changed my mind.

"Paperback tours are much different from hardcover tours. You don't really sell and autograph that many books on tours, and there isn't much pussy on the paperback tours, unless you're into fat little broads who work at Safeway.

"On the hardcover tours, I've spent too much time apologizing to bookstore owners, who are also frustrated writers, why *I* got a decent deal while the bookstore owner, if he was to get published at all, had to settle for that online self-publishing bullshit. Sometimes I'll sit in the store and drink a cappuccino and show the shoppers where the computer books are. On this paperback tour, I'll wander into the nearest supermarket and occasionally someone will recognize me and they'll ask me to pose for a cell phone picture.

"Painless banged you up pretty bad, eh? Maybe that's a good thing. You can hang up your helmet and join Al Michaels in the broadcast booth."

"Piros was telling me that a bit earlier."

"Then do it. You don't want to stay in football anyway. It sucks now," he said.

"I still love it. I want to play some more."

"Do the broadcasting. Al Michaels will like you. You may even end up hawking Heineken or Corona on TV."

"But I drink Canadian Comfort," I reminded him.

"When you feel better, we'll get good and pissed on Canadian Comfort over ice."

"How's your book selling?"

"Doesn't matter. I don't need the money."

Our conversation ended a few minutes later. Flash didn't cheer me up as much as he usually did.

Was it really true what the doctors were saying? Was I too badly injured to continue playing football?

Aside from playing football, I was what one might call unemployable. I could talk clever shit during a brief on-air interview, but what did I know about doing color during an actual full-length game?

I sank into a deep funk for close to an hour, convinced that I would never find gratifying work again nor receive inflated paychecks. My iPhone rang again and I muttered, "Yeah?"

"Just 'yeah'? Is that any way to answer your phone?" I smiled at the sound of Sheri's voice. "Anyway, I saw how Painless and those bullies roughed you up. Hope they didn't put your love muscle on the disabled list."

"No, sweetness, some of me still works fine."

TWO

Someone once told me that marriage was a year of heaven followed by two decades of hell. He added that if you decided to stay in that marriage when it became hellish, you deserved what you got.

I don't think my Uncle Rex told me that. He married and divorced often, and he didn't stay with any of his wives long enough to figure out if he could tolerate her for two decades.

Uncle Rex showed very little emotion when his wives left him. He just smoked a Player's Light as they stormed out, wagging their middle fingers at him.

"There goes Lonnie," he would say. "Lord help the next poor dumb bastard who takes up with her."

Uncle Rex had raised me in his Bayporte house, so I lived with his tramps. I remember some better than others. Wendy had red hair and the temper of a rabid pit bull. Frederica went bananas with Uncle Rex's credit cards. Patti had a retarded brother we loved to mock. Louise cranked up the volume on the stereo and boogied about the living room in her undies. Loretta had psychiatric problems; she went on and off every kind of medication.

All of his wives knew how to cook a variety of dishes and had full-time jobs. Most of them sat at computers and tapped on keys till Carpal-Tunnel syndrome made their wrists burn, while others spent their days in banks, being nice to rude people.

I wondered why Uncle Rex kept getting hitched when all of his marriages seemed doomed from the start. I asked him about it one day while he studied the racing form at his favorite downtown pool hall.

"Oh, I don't know, Red," he said. "I guess it's Woody's fault. He gets me into nothing but trouble."

Woody was the nickname of Uncle Rex's penis.

. . .

My mum and dad said *no mas* while I was still in kindergarten. As Uncle Rex put it, "Your dad unfolded a gas station road map and drew a vertical line through Canada. He said to your mum, 'I'll take this half and you can have the other half.'

"Your mum said, 'Are you sure half of Canada will be enough? Will there be enough blonde bimbos to keep you happy?'

"Your dad said, 'Yeah, I'll be on the lookout for just those girls, even though I like your pot belly and saggy bum.'

"'Asshole!' your mum screamed. 'If you don't get punished for your awful ways, it'll be because God pities fools like you!'

"Your dad said, 'At least God has given me enough common sense to get the fuck away from you!'

"'That right, eh?' your mum said. 'At least now I won't have a husband who humiliates me by chasing every slut in town!'"

They gave me a choice: I could go to Ontario with Dad or to Victoria with Mum and watch as she searched for a new hubby. Although I don't remember saying so, apparently I told them, "I want to move in with Uncle Rex. He loves sports as much as I do and he doesn't fight with anyone."

Mum took off, and I didn't see her again.

In Victoria, she remarried and had two or three more children. She sent me ten dollars for each birthday. She died, during my adolescence, from a broken neck when her children, as a joke, pushed her down the stairs, and she hit the landing head first.

Uncle Rex took me to her funeral.

This was my first time at such an event, but I figured out that the man in the first row who wore a down vest and a Labatt's Blue cap, was my stepfather, Al. We said nothing to each other.

I saw my dad only one more time after he moved to Ontario. I was a football stud at Northup by then. The Kodiaks had flown to Toronto to play against the University of Toronto Blues. Flash, Sheri and I were standing in the lobby of our hotel, killing time as we waited for our bus to take us to the football field. We laughed at all the tourists in their I LOVE TORONTO souvenir clothing, aiming their iPhones at each other. Then a man came towards us, and I thought at first he was another football fan who wanted to meet Flash and me.

"Hi, Red," he said. "I'm your dad."

"Identify yourself," Flash interjected.

"I'm Fred Crossley," he said.

"What was the name of Red's mum?" asked Sheri.

"Madge," said Fred.

Sheri shrugged. "Good enough for me."

I took Fred aside to spare him the humiliation of Sheri's wisecracks. He told me he had followed my "heroics" online. He told me he had meant to write to me several times over the years but that "life got in the way."

He looked around the lobby and saw some of my teammates. "Lots of blackies on your team, hey?"

I shrugged. "Some."

"No worse than Chinks or Pakis, I guess."

"They're OK," I said. "Good guys."

"They don't steal from you, I hope."

"Never," I told him.

"Do they borrow money from you?"

"I borrow from them," I said.

"The other day," my father told me, "I saw a one of them in the afternoon haul out his dingus and piss on Yonge Street! Can you believe it?"

"Shame on him."

"Yes! Right there in downtown Toronto, like he thought it was OK to do that! I thought, 'Well, this may be the beginning of the end of life as we know it, when a spade pisses in the street and then goes about his merry way.' Just too bad, eh?"

"I guess that's the way it goes."

He said he was sorry for taking off and leaving me in the care of Uncle Rex.

"You have nothing to apologize for," I said. "Uncle Rex helped me to develop a good attitude. Plus, we laughed our asses off practically every day of the year."

"I was sorry to hear about your mum. I know she wasn't happy with me but she had a happy life with someone else. I wish she would have lived longer."

"You remarried, too, right?"

He nodded. "Couple of times. They were both violent, crazy women, which isn't necessarily a bad thing. But I've learned my lesson. No more wives."

My father died a couple of years later on a golf course when a single-engine Cessna crashed into some nearby trees. He had been so engrossed in grooving his swing that he apparently couldn't hear the yells and shouts from people to get out of the way.

Dear old Dad did not claim to be Dr. Laura or Dr.

Joy Browne, but in that hotel lobby that day, he told me something I will always remember.

"Red, I'm no genius; if I was, I wouldn't be selling laminated flooring for a living," he'd said. "I know you play a tough game with a bunch of tough guys, but let me say this one thing: You haven't been bruised and battered till you've had a wife who was mad at you."

. . .

Considering how much boredom I had to cope with in that hospital bed, one couldn't really blame me for the weird things that spun through my mind.

I watched countless old patients traipse past my room and told myself: You will become one of them or die first. Take your pick.

I wondered how many patients our nurse inadvertently killed through negligence. She pulled at her hair and rolled her eyes every time I saw her. I heard her holler, "This place is gonna make me start drinking again!"

But mainly I thought about all the difficulties and challenges of married life.

As I lay there in my room at Bayporte General Hospital—me, my wounded brain and my iPad—I ruminated on being in my thirties. Most of the people I knew had been divorced at least once.

One of the exceptions, Lord Larry and Lady Joy Rawson—Sheri's parents—had pissed each other off a zillion times, but would have never considered splitting up. "They'll never call it quits," Sheri told me. "If they got a divorce, it would make them feel they were no better than everybody else, and they've *always* felt inherently superior. Besides," she added, "Mum and her lawyers would take forever to figure out where Dad's hid all his money."

Flash Gortton, once said to me, "I would rather be locked up for twenty years with Charles Manson and Jeffrey Dahmer than go looking for furniture with a woman roomie."

Davy Carpenter had left his share of wives. I still felt angry at him for handing off to me and sending me right at Painless, who sent me right into this hospital room. If Davy had been as bad a quarterback as he had been a husband, he would've botched that handoff, the referee would have blown the play dead and I would walking around and enjoying life instead of lying here like an invalid, holding my iPad and trying to read a *People* article about an aging movie actor who had "found God" and prayed to Him nightly to deliver the parts he coveted.

Carpenter held one NFL record that nobody wanted to tie. He had married two flight attendants and as many Invaders cheerleaders. I found out about his latest divorce on TV.

The newsmagazine show *Canada This Week* had learned that the Great White North's most progressive city, Bayporte, had become home to a handful of drive-through divorce centers in which newly graduated lawyers handled over a hundred ten-minute divorces each day. I lay in bed, watching the program with some amusement, when Davy Carpenter appeared onscreen with his latest ex, Toni.

"It's a sad day for us," he said. "I said to her so many times, 'We're gonna make it, baby.'"

"How long were you married?" the reporter asked Toni.

"About a week," she replied.

"About a week?" the reporter exclaimed. "Why such

a brief marriage?"

Toni shrugged and ran a hand through her blonde hair. "Gee, I don't know. I guess the vibrations just weren't right."

How could love survive in such a brutal world? I lay in my hospital bed and nearly wept. Love, like me, was on the disabled list; and love, unlike me, needed to live forever. Perhaps love had survived wars and depressions and, if anything, come out stronger than before. But give people money and boredom, and love was in big fucking trouble.

When we were younger, Sheri would have agreed with me that nothing—especially the things that money bought—could destroy our love. We, and our love, were too smart. But some of those fancy, shiny things *did* compromise us—they said to us, "We're more important to you than you are to each other"—and we had to admit it: We were humans, no better than everyone else.

Nothing in our experience had prepared us for the humbling realization that we were merely human. Our experience, in fact, had convinced us that we didn't have to worry about becoming merely human.

Sheri, Flash and I had become friends in the third grade. That year, we had formed our own little clique, a society dedicated to pitying everyone not fortunate enough to be named Sheri, Flash or Red.

We laughed at the crap sandwiches other kids had to eat at McIntosh Elementary. Then we mocked the clothing those kids had to wear, and the parents who made them wear it. Soon we got to the point where we believed that everything in life was too ludicrous to take seriously, especially the serious things.

As we grew up, the three of us shared a set of beliefs on the big issues: Learning, achieving, surviving. As I recall, we developed most of our beliefs through observing adults.

We agreed that each person had an obligation, to himself and the rest of the world, to recognize his gifts as soon as possible and nurture them throughout his lifetime.

We believed that we should enjoy our favorite songs and movies but not emulate the bad boys and girls those songs and movies glorified.

We promised each other we wouldn't hurt others on our ascent to the pinnacle of worldly success, but conceded that a little backtalk was all right if the other person deserved it.

We agreed that the main thing in life was what you *did* and how you treated others, not who you were, what you had or how you looked.

We concluded that the only people worth trusting were those who had attended Oliver Johnson Secondary School.

We maintained that a footlong steak-and-salami special and a bottle of pop at Paul's Submarine Sandwich Stop was a far finer meal than any dish that had gotten four stars in the *Michelin Guide*.

We embraced all of these notions when we came of age, and clung to our ideology even more as we graduated from Northup University and got ready to play professional football.

Flash and I vowed to play for the same team, preferably for the NFL—ideally for the Bayporte

Invaders—but we'd sign with a CFL team if necessary. Fortunately, the NFL and CFL considered us pretty hot stuff, and we had an "ally, mentor and confidant" in Lord Larry Rawson, who had countless connections and could get us whatever we wanted.

"I'm in business," Lord Larry had told us. "Minerals, oil, cattle—I'm into everything. Right now, though, I'm in the business of making sure that you two boys end up with the Invaders, if that's what you want. If those boys at NuWest Sports say no to you, that's the same as saying no to *me*, and I don't think they're that dumb."

The Bayporte Invaders ultimately agreed to accept Flash and me, mainly because NuWest Sports knew what Lord Larry wanted.

The Bayporte Invaders made me their first-round draft pick, and when the Miami Dolphins selected Flash, the Invaders offered Miami a future Number One draft pick and some money in exchange for Flash Gortton.

Sheri, Flash and I moved in together. Her parents thought we had ourselves quite a peculiar domestic arrangement, but Sheri, as usual, showed little interest in how they felt about what their daughter did. By then, Sheri was deeply in love with Flash, or maybe just infatuated and unaware of the difference between having creamy panties for someone or experiencing genuine, honest-to-God man-woman love.

The three of us shacked up at the Hotel Bayporte while Sheri searched for a permanent residence where we would all be comfortable. Soon she found a condominium for sale overlooking Pioneer Park and Sailor Bay.

"The place has four balconies and a pair of

fireplaces," she said.

"Yeah, that'll do." The condo had a living room big enough to hold all of our friends and admirers.

Sheri had majored in journalism at Northup, one of the few Canadian colleges with a journalism department. Once she graduated, she sought an entry-level reporter job but ended up modeling.

Suddenly, we saw her on billboards and bus boards, in magazines and on television. In those ads, her tacit message never varied: Smoke these cigarettes, drink this booze, wash your hair with this shampoo and stay at this hotel and maybe you'll become just like me or get to fuck someone just like me.

So Sheri became a high-priced model, receiving huge paychecks she scarcely needed. Flash and I expected her to succeed at whatever she did. She was so drop-dead gorgeous that men and women, checking her out as they walked past her, ended up colliding on the sidewalk. In a pair of tight Levi's and a snug sweatshirt, she all but stopped traffic as she walked down Royal Avenue and flashed her Pepsi smile at all passersby. And why shouldn't she smile, with her strawberry blonde hair tumbling about her shoulders and plump breasts bouncing in the fresh Canadian air?

Like most other beautiful women, she could have grooved through life just on her looks. Plus, her daddy had more money than his daughter could have spent in a dozen lifetimes. But Sheri had *so* much more going for her, so many admirable qualities: ebullience, street wisdom, erudition, a sense of humor and irony. A mistress of backtalk, she owned a lethal tongue.

Unlike most other models, Sheri had intelligence, a quality which prevented her from respecting modeling. She showed us her paychecks and watched as Flash and I blanched with envy. Sheri waxed philosophical about her ambivalence towards modeling and the money she got from it.

"Look, if the agencies want to pay me this much to wear their dress to the party, I'd be a fucking fool not to do it. Right?" Adding, "I'm what you would call a high-priced hooker. But one who doesn't have to fuck anybody. Isn't that the best kind of hooker to be?"

One evening, while the three of us were hanging out in our condo, Flash teased Sheri a bit.

"Admit it," he said, "you, as a model, are important to our economy. You create demand. When you endorse something, it's because you believe your product is superior. Soon enough, the inferior products become unavailable, and you've singlehandedly strengthened the economy."

Sheri thought about this for a minute. Then she said, "Flash, you're so full of shit."

· · ·

Through the years of Flash and Sheri's on-again, off-again love affair, I played the part of their good buddy and tidy roomie. I searched through Bayporte and a dozen other cities for a Sheri to call my own, but Flash had the only one.

Sheri, damn the bitch, withheld the approval she knew I needed whenever I brought by a girlfriend. Yes, Sheri would be polite enough if I was in the middle of a romance, but would never actually say, "Damn! Cristina is a real sweetie!" or "Wow! Kari is such fun to hang out with!"

Sheri would be tactful. Great word, eh? She would be absolutely, completely tactful.

Our days and nights had hilarity and silliness when Flash, Sheri and I would go out with some girl, or stay in together, or even take a trip. Occasionally the girl would be someone really special whom Sheri might add to her own circle of friends. But inevitably my relationship with that girl would be doomed after I got Sheri's feedback on her.

Sometimes I would actually solicit such feedback, but even if I didn't, Sheri would speak up. One word, maybe two, but devastating all the same.

The feedback would destroy the relationship, for how could I love a woman if Sheri disapproved of her? She might be a magnificent specimen of womanhood, beautiful and kind and brilliant, but Sheri's rapier wit would turn her into an AIDS-infected retarded freak I wished I had never met.

Sheri had done this to me in high school. Johane Meehan was a great catch in every way. However, one evening at Paul's Submarine Sandwich Stop, as Flash, Sheri and I sat around—an activity all Bayporters take *very* seriously—I did something stupid. I went on for a bit about Johane's good points.

"Electra," Sheri said.

I looked up from my sandwich. "Excuse me?"

"I was just thinking about the Electra complex," she said. "Daddy's girl. Johane seems very attached to her father, hey?"

After Johane, I had a nice time with Pinky Goebbels, a cheerleader whose talent for grinding her butt guaranteed sold-out games. I terminated my relationship with Pinky after Sheri offered me a three-word appraisal of my newest lady love.

"She needs braces."

During our final year in high school, I became involved with Kathy Curry. Kathy, a major cutie, had a cool detachment that I admired. She dressed with flair and imagination.

"You like her a lot, right?" Sheri asked.

"She's the woman I love," I replied. "Got a problem with that?"

"She's very pretty," Sheri said, nodding. "However—"

I frowned. "What?"

"Well, it's just that—"

"Come on. Spit it out," I told her.

She shrugged. "Closet dyke."

Another one bit the dust. Sheri did that to me all through Northup and into the Invaders.

Only a chump would have stopped seeing some of the voluptuous playmates who made my nights a bit less lonely. But Sheri's terse dismissals spoiled my enjoyment of those ladies the moment they left her mouth.

Deanna Rae?

"Freckles."

Cheryl Artus?

"Versacc."

Gloria Lodge?

"Hippie."

Lydia Neufeld?

"Hypocrite."

Katy Wood?

"Airhead."

Sarah Burditt?

"Rhinoplasty."

Heather Stafford?

"Blimp."

Ginny Worley?

"Illiterate."

Melissa Price?

"Slut."

Tracy Montagne?

"Bulimic."

One time, I maintained a relationship for a couple of months before letting Sheri destroy it for me. I had started my second season with the Invaders when I fell in love with Kristin Alkins.

I had first seen her on TV. They introduced her as their newest sports reporter, and at first I thought she might have been one of Sheri's Northup journalism classmates. But no; she probably didn't even have a high school diploma.

Kristin Alkins, a staggering beauty, had long dark hair and eyes the color of cobalt. She also had a magnificent, flawless body.

I called her up and asked her out during her first week on the air. I found something seductive about how she read the news. When she said, "A dozen Asian gangsters wiped out as many Indian rivals early this morning in eastern Bayporte," what I heard her say was, "Put your cock in me and start pumping away."

Kris, always sexy and alluring, also had ample intelligence and charisma. She was vivacious and earthy, always down to have a good time. Flash admired her almost as much as I did. Sheri liked her, too—at least for the first couple of months.

Then I fucked it all up. I pretty much dared Sheri to find one objectionable thing about Kris. The three of us—Sheri, Flash and I—sat in a Bayporte bar and I boasted, long and loud, about Kris's beauty, charm and intelligence.

Sheri cut me down with one word.

"Cider."

Those two little syllables came out gently, but her eyes gleamed in victory as she spoke them.

I stared into my drink for a moment, as if the retort I sought floated about in that glass of Canadian Comfort and ice chips. I gave up and stared off into space, wondering for the briefest moment if I should be offended that the other bar patrons seemed indifferent to the presence of Flash and me. Mainly, however, I tried to cope with the knowledge that Kris Alkins drank nothing but Great Elizabeth Sparkling Cider, an odious, mildly alcoholic beverage that probably tasted, and certainly smelled, like apple pop.

I did not call it quits with her the next day. We gradually allowed our relationship to rot and blacken until it dissolved into little bits of nothing that floated away. Once I was through with her, Flash said I seemed like a famished mongoose after a prolonged tussle with a big cobra. A weasel that had scurried away, unbitten but unfed, dusty and humbled.

Some of our friends said that Sheri had spared me many years of *tsuris*. Maybe they were right. I learned soon that Kris Alkins cared far more about her career than she ever could have cared about me.

She bedded down with the right people and got the promotion she sought as the weekend anchor at the Northern Broadcasting Company's affiliate in Toronto. While there, she became the girlfriend of a married Member of Parliament; he flew her to Ottawa for nooners at the taxpayers' expense. Later, she married, then divorced, a Toronto publishing magnate. While they were together, they moved to Hollywood so he could expand his business empire. After their divorce, she attended all the right parties and rode all the right dicks to procure a production job with a major studio. I read on one of the online gossip sites that she had gotten herself happily ensconced in a big Hollywood Hills condo.

Not to brag, but I can honestly say that I kept my hands off Sheri as long as she and Flash were a couple. Certainly, I longed for her throughout countless nights as she slept two dozen feet away.

Sheri, possessor of every attractive and admirable trait I believed a woman could have, became the sole reason I searched so long and hard for someone comparable to her. But only when she and Flash acknowledged that their relationship was beginning to end did I look upon her as my next lover.

Sheri and Flash concluded, by the time we were pushing thirty, that the two of them would be lifelong close friends but little else. Soon after we won the Super Bowl, Flash made the huge decision that he wanted to retire from football and explore the world alone. He told Sheri that, as his twenty-ninth birthday approached, he had accomplished much yet done so little. He hadn't even started composing the Great Canadian Novel, and he needed to have adventures that would broaden his horizons and give him something to write about. Also, he wanted to boff some foreign women.

We sat in the darkest section of a Bayporte bar as

Flash told Sheri of his plans.

"This is something I have to do for myself, *by* myself," he told her. "Besides, I want to find out if it's true what they say about Asian women."

"Like what? That they make your bed after you're done banging them?" asked Sheri.

"It's just that I need to go there and check out the rest of the world. I'm too narrow. I must absorb some culture."

"You have this thing about wanting to be everywhere except where you are," Sheri said.

Flash sucked down his glass of Canadian Comfort, signaled for a refill and said, "Sheri, sweetie, you know that you're my number-one gal. Always have been, always will be. But you know I have this character flaw about being unable to be with just one woman. As fine a fuck as you've been, I'd always be looking for another contortionist."

"Wilbert," Sheri said, calling him by his given name, "do you want to know what I see? I see you back here in twenty years, all tuckered out from years of wandering the planet. You'd be walking these streets, shaking your head at how much everything had changed and calling yourself a fool for having left your home in search of something that didn't exist."

"I wouldn't be lonely," he said, "if there was a decent person somewhere who was willing to talk to me. Besides, no matter where I am or what I'm doing, I'll always have you and Red, even if you're not present physically."

Flash ran off to Europe for a few months. He spent most of his time hanging out in England, learning firsthand about life. "They sure talk funny over here," he told us in an email. "I think you two know that you've always been in love. Sheri, you got involved with me only because you knew you could have Red whenever you wanted him, and I've always been OK with that.

"You have a powerful attraction to each other's privates, but have resisted the urge to jump on each other only out of respect for me. Well, I'm here and you're there, so I think you should start balling immediately, if you haven't already done so.

"Red, we need to keep Sheri in our little family. You know how many dirty old men are out there, trying to get into her snatch. Alas, I've never been the marrying type, but you are. Get a ring on her finger and a lock on her box.

"You will definitely find dating each other awkward at first, considering you've been more like siblings throughout your lives. Go slowly at first, like holding hands and going to movies. Then, on some evening, when you get back to the apartment, try going down on each other till you scream."

I had to admit that Flash had a point about the awkwardness of going from platonic to romantic. It seemed an awful lot like screwing the sister I'd never had.

Also, I wasn't altogether sure we were "dating." Much of the time, I thought of us as roomies and lifelong pals who dined and drank together on most nights. Sheri, of course, saw other men, but usually just to talk business over dinner. Then she would skedaddle home to Yours Truly.

One evening, we got falling-down drunk and groped our way through a lovemaking session. Sheri ordered me out of her bedroom the moment I looked as though I might actually penetrate her. She also didn't like how I kept talking about my former girlfriends while I was supposed to be pleasuring her.

Things changed for us one evening when we decided to stay home to give our livers a chance to recover from our recent debauchery. We lay sprawled out on a couple of sofas in the living room, watching the fire. I'd put on a Jeter Davis CD and, as always, felt comforted by the sound of my old friend's voice.

Sheri took me by surprise as she jumped on me.

"I want us to try something new," she said, snaking her arms around my neck.

"You gonna hurt me? Don't hurt me. I've been hurt a lot."

"Oh, baby, just you shut your mouth," she said. "Don't laugh or smile. Don't say anything about Oliver Johnson High or Northup University. If you say one word, I'll sever your jugular. Nod if you understand."

I nodded.

Then she kissed me in a way I still find difficult to describe.

I returned her kiss, using everything I had ever learned about kissing. Our kiss lasted eons and left both of our tongues disabled. Then we went out and got married.

Our ceremony happened in a chapel of the Northup University Christian Church, just across the street from the campus. We had an informal ceremony and took our guests for a free lunch at Paul's Submarine Sandwich Stop.

Flash Gortton, who'd been out wandering Mother Earth, flew back home to be my best man. He even offered to be Sheri's maid of honor. Lord Larry gave her away and made sure that the preacher got paid.

Lady Joy postponed her day's shopping to be with us. My Uncle Rex showed up mainly because he had nothing better to do.

As I say, we had a small guest list. The minister blessed everyone at Northup and most of the people in Bayporte. He blessed Lord Larry's businesses and hoped Jesus wasn't too offended by the worldwide state of affairs. He forgave the Chinks, Pakis and queers for corrupting society, then he pronounced Sheri and me man and wife.

As I say, we had our reception at Paul's Submarine Sandwich Stop.

Paul's, our hangout since we were minors, was our favorite place because we knew that Paul would serve us Diefenbaker beer even though we were underage. Paul made the biggest, juiciest sandwiches in town. He bought only the freshest ingredients, and we didn't mind the nonstop chatter, clatter and grease.

After Sheri and I traded rings and kissed, we and our guests arrived at Paul's in our fine clothing. He laughed and congratulated us as our guests sneered at our beloved, mostly vacant greasy spoon. My bride and I devoured succulent steak sandwiches, guzzled down countless bottles of Dief, punched in our requests on the jukebox—yes, Paul had one, although it, like his restaurant, would disappear a few years later—and danced in the restaurant.

Lady Joy afterwards reiterated her disappointment over her only child's refusal of a traditional, lavish society wedding, considering the Rawsons' affluence and social status. Paula Jansen's wedding gown was magnificent, Lady Joy said. Their reception had been unforgettable. Alanis Morissette had flown up to serenade the couple.

"Well, what of it?" Sheri said to her mum. "Paula Jansen is a cunt and her husband is a prick. They'll be divorced within a few years."

Lord Larry said he felt relieved that Sheri had married me. "For a time, I was afraid you and Flash and Sheri were into one of those three-way kinky things."

If anyone had asked me, "How do you manage to keep these old, close friendships alive?" I would have answered, "By not working at it." Most people don't have close friends; and many don't have any friends at all, if your definition of *friend* is similar to mine. Those without close friends alienate everyone by bitching nonstop about ME ME ME ME ME. The glue that had held Flash, Sheri and me together since childhood must have seemed a very curious compound to Lord Larry, but to the three of us our love or friendship, or whatever we had, was just natural and special. It needed no tending or maintaining.

We rarely thought we were unusual in how much we loved, helped, empathized with, forgave and protected each other. As the song went, that's what friends are for. That's what families are for, too, so I guess I've always considered us a family of three.

Over the next several years, Sheri and I screwed like rabbits, yet still managed to make an appearance at every party to which we had been invited.

I continued to be known and admired all over town despite the Invaders' poor record and my recent emasculation by—marriage to—Sheri Rawson, who had kept her name.

We wanted Flash to move back in with us after our honeymoon. Amazingly, he agreed. "Being homeless," as he put it, "is starting to bore me." While he figured out what to do next, he spent endless hours in his bedroom, typing on his MacBook Pro.

"Writers," he reminded us, "need to obsess a lot. Plus, we need plenty of room for our gadgets while we write about our obsessions."

Sheri and I, lovers in love, made out in public places and giggled at each other for no reason. Like characters in a love story, we wanted to have snowball fights, ride horses and watch parades as Itzhak Perlman played his violin nearby.

Whenever Sheri and I would get too lovey-dovey, I would imagine Flash saying, "Cut! Get ready for take two. We need some schmaltzy music, too."

Flash inevitably became the guy with a bevy of beauties. But unlike me, he was indifferent to Sheri's feedback.

Sheri sometimes had trouble making small talk with Flash's girlfriends.

One night Flash brought by a Judy or an Amber, some vapid cutie who aspired to work as a Canadian Airways flight attendant, model or actress. The four of us sat at our favorite downtown Bayporte bar.

We covered a number of topics and Judy or Amber listened with much patience or boredom. She spoke up only once, to ask if we thought that story about Richard Gere and the gerbils was true.

Sheri made an attempt at engaging Judy or Amber in conversation. Leaning across the table, sipping a freshly poured Canadian Comfort over ice, Sheri stared into the bimbo's wide, spacy gray eyes. "Swimming, snorkeling, skiing? Skydiving?"

The girl frowned. "Excuse me?"

"What's your thing, girlfriend? What do you like to do?"

The girl's eyebrows started knitting a sweater, as if she'd just been asked, by Socrates himself, to define life.

The girl brightened up and said, "Shopping! *That's* my thing!"

Sheri spat out her mouthful of Canadian Comfort and ran off to the ladies' room, her laughter audible to everyone in the bar.

Our four years of marriage were the happiest of my life, not counting football. I decided that if I couldn't be King of the Universe, the next best thing was to be the husband of Sheri Rawson.

Then TV happened to me.

Now, back to that night in early fall as I lay in my Bayporte hospital bed, still wobbly and angry at my wife for being in Los Angeles instead of at my bedside and sounding over the telephone as if she were doing just fine without me.

After her question about my love muscle, Sheri said, "I didn't see the game. We were in the studio all day and when I peeked into the control room, they had something else on.

"Westwood House is better than I expected," she said. "This is the hotel the hippest Hollywood types stay at ever since the industrialists and dentists have invaded most of the Beverly Hills hotels."

"You missed the game, eh? Too bad," I said.

"How long will you be on the disabled list?"

I gave a small, bitter laugh. "The old career is up, sweetie. My brain is telling me, 'That concussion hurt. I'm through with this bullshit."

I heard her sigh. Then, "Oh, well. All you need now is to make a career change. Go on TV."

"People keep saying that," I muttered.

"Well, it would be easy enough for you. Just say what you always say when you're watching a football game. I just hope the Americans can understand your Canuck accent."

"I'd rather suit up and kick ass on the football field."

"I don't think that option is still on the table," Sheri said. "You should approach the networks and see who'll pay you the most."

"Ho hum," I muttered.

"Do you hurt much?"

"Only when I think, breathe or talk."

"My poor baby."

"Your poor baby just wants to get out of here and go home. Ugh."

"I'm not that far away. I can fly up there and we can spend the whole day together. They won't mind if I take a day off. Actually, they'll get pissed off, but screw 'em."

"Don't do it, Sheri," I told her.

"But I want to spend a day with you."

"Stay there so your bosses won't get mad. After my discharge, maybe I'll fly down there and bug you for a while."

"Sweetness," Sheri said, "you know how much I want to be up there with you to help you through this trying time. But I have people down here who are depending on me. This pilot we're shooting? It all sort of revolves around me."

"Then stay down there," I said.

"Do you mean that?"

"Yes," I lied. Then, "I wouldn't want your Hollywood bosses to get mad. They'd come up here and bludgeon me to death with their Oscars."

Sheri's gentle tone now became impatient. "Come *on*, Red. I'm making the best of a bad situation. You stay up there and take it easy. We'll get together as often as possible."

"How often? Once a year?"

"Don't be like that. I know you feel awful. Your career is over, you have a killer headache and you're not too keen on this broadcasting thing. But remember what will happen if I stay down here and complete this pilot. What if the pilot becomes a major hit? Do you have any idea how much money it would be worth? How much it would improve our lives?"

"Money?" I asked. "We already have that."

"We could have lots more if this TV show goes for me. I could buy you your own football team. What would you call it?"

"I don't want a fuckin' football team. I just want my wife back."

Sheri sighed. "Your wife is getting sick of the idiot scripts she's getting. The latest one came in this morning. Unfortunately it's not *Roseanne* or even *Moesha*, but the producers think it has a certain *Je ne sais quoi*. Tomorrow they'll say it's *dreck* but I have to be a trouper and do the best with the material they give me. Right? It's not my fault that they're spending millions of dollars for bad scripts and that this whole project may just be a big waste of time, is it? Well, you know me. I'm a professional."

"Yes," I said. "You're a professional. You have your priorities straight."

"That's good, right?"

"Affirmative."

She said, "I'll call you every hour. Maybe every few hours. It depends on how many takes we have to do."

"I thought there was more to big-time TV than doing takes. Don't you guys eat at those hip joints where they serve fish pizza?"

She laughed.

"Isn't it weird," I said, "that they can't get a decent script despite having a dozen writers and millions of dollars to pay them?"

"Yes, it's weird. Let's just be patient. When you feel better, you can come down here and bug me all you want. The smog will do you good."

"Will you take me on a tour of the studio? Will you introduce me to some movie stars? Will you take me to Disneyland and buy me a pair of Mickey Mouse ears?"

"Whatever you want," Sheri told me. "Just make sure you're feeling well. I don't know how long I'll be here. These TV pilots are crazy things. If ours gets picked up, we'll have to start taping episodes *tout de suite*. But that's all in the future. You need to recover. Eat and sleep lots. Don't worry if you gain a few pounds."

"OK, Mum."

We hung up the phone after my meds kicked in and I got muzzy. "Sheri," I said, "I don't want to fight with you. You're too tough—you'd kick my ass in two minutes."

THREE

Painless O'Neal flew out to Bayporte to visit me in the hospital, but he came to see me for reasons other than saying hidy.

"Sorry I hit you so hard. Hope you get better soon. We gotta have your support, Red." Painless bounced a bit on his feet, as he usually did when fearing he might not get his own way. "The union needs you more than you know. You're a credit to the NFL. If you say strike, many other players will do it just because you think it's a good idea."

Painless, Number Two Man in the NFL Players' Association, seemed to have everything but always wanted something else. At this moment, what he craved even more than another vintage Rolex or Cadillac, was a players' strike.

He wanted players to do whatever they would be doing if they weren't playing, even if they had to take jobs as coal miners and factory workers.

Hardly for the first time in his career, Painless wanted every player on every team in the National Football League to go on strike. All of them. Every one. He wanted us all to get on a picket line and stay there until the owners agreed to offer us more money and other goodies.

I had always considered a strike to be a poor idea. Painless, Pol Pott and I had argued about this issue. In my mind, a strike had little chance of success. "If we grab them by the balls, they'll just cut off our hands, if you understand my metaphor."

"We got leverage, baby," Painless said. "You would be our spokesman. One of our spokesmen, anyway."

"No can do, guy. The owners are all filthy rich. If we all quit, they'll just get new players."

"They need *us*. The fans are in love with Red Crossley, Painless O'Neal—"

"Like hell they are. The fans are in love with whoever is rushing into the end zone. Flash Gortton quit recently and they're already forgetting who he was."

Painless pointed his finger at me and said, "Do you know how many guys are ready to go on strike? Well over half. If more upper-echelon guys like you came onboard, we'd have a very viable work stoppage ready to happen."

"Painless," I said, "how much money do you have in the bank? Even if you sold your cars and bling, you wouldn't have nearly enough to live on. The teams are just another investment item to the owners; they don't give a shit who stays and who walks. If you strike, better look for a new career, and tell the other players that applies to them, too. The players who deal steroids will still make money, but everyone else will be fucked."

He tsked. "Champ, you don't got this figured right. Poor people don't have money, so when they get some, they piss it all away on something they like. But rich people are different. They *hate* to lose money. They think it's a gift from God or something and that He meant it for *them* and no one else." He paused. "Besides, the everyday sports fan would take our side."

I cackled. "The everyday sports fan thinks Joe

Montana is going to make a comeback. The average sports fan just wants someone to cheer for and bet on."

"Red, you know you could double your salary as a free agent. Right?"

"Painless, *you* know I no longer have a football career. Right? My head hurts and I need to find a new occupation. You know what that's all about?"

"Yeah, I know. What we're trying to do is get a salary scale that pays us what we're worth, not the chump change the owners want to pay us."

"I know that. I read where you said that your demands were not negotiable. Nice way to bargain, eh?"

Painless shrugged. "A sports reporter sticks his microphone in your face and asks, 'What's goin' on?' You tell him straight up. He hears it, the rest of the world hears it, the owners hear it. You need to show the world you're not a pussy or a wimp. You need to show everyone that you've got a pair." He added, "We need to strike now to get the full free-market value for what we do."

I laughed. "Gee, Painless, all this time I thought we played because of our love for the game." As he departed, I said, "Do me a big favor. Before you start the strike, give me the name of your financial counselor."

They were right about TV. That very day, an ESPN guy called and offered me lots of money to sit in a broadcast booth, put on s headset and flap my gums.

The following day, that suit flew in to meet me in person.

He told me he was Mark Richardson, president of ESPN, and I guessed that he was so new as Number One Man that the ink on his business cards was still wet. He sat by my bed and polished his glasses.

A svelte man in his mid-thirties, he wore a dark suit, white shirt and striped tie. His fair hair was cut too short and his smooth face betrayed no humor. He probably ran marathons, ate a vegan diet and had no fun at all.

He spoke of what *I* could do for *him*, not what *he* could do for *me*. In some very weird way, I respected him for being up front about that.

"Getting Red Crossley aboard would be my first accomplishment as the boss," he said. "It would force the network to take me seriously."

Over the previous two years, ESPN had gone through three presidents, all of them attorneys like Mark Richardson.

"I know all about television, live or tape, and I have a vision of what ESPN could and should be," he said as I admired his manicured fingernails. "Did you like Summerall and Madden?"

"Yes. I also like Al Michaels and John Madden," I told him.

"I was partly responsible for putting Madden and Summerall together," Mark Richardson told me. "The idea was to combine Summerall's matter-of-fact seriousness with Madden's crude wisdom and informed intelligence."

"'Informed intelligence,'" I said, "is a good thing."

"You have potential, Red. You seem to have presence and you're currently popular. Plus, if you signed with us, we would team you up with Con Horwitz."

Con Horwitz, perhaps the worst announcer in sports broadcasting history, had the goofiest hairpiece and the most superficial knowledge of sports. If he was covering a game where the score was 49-0 in the fourth quarter and the team with 0 recovered a fumble and ran it back for a touchdown, Conrad would yell, "They're making a comeback! They're making a comeback! Can you believe it?"

Of course, I didn't say any of this to the man who could pay me good money to fly to a handful of cities, get drunk on Canadian Comfort over ice and talk football on Sunday.

This is what I said to Mark Richardson: "Con Horwitz is a very experienced broadcaster."

"He certainly is." Mark leaned over and offered me an Excel mint. "Naturally, I would like for Con to get fewer statistics wrong while he's on the air, but everyone knows who he is just by looking at or listening to him, and in TV that matters a great deal."

"Many of my friends don't like him. They want him to give the time and score and not much more," I said.

"He doesn't appeal to everyone," Richardson conceded. Then, "Who's your agent?"

"You're looking at him."

He frowned. "You represent yourself? Really?"

I shrugged. "Why not?"

He frowned some more. "How can you be without an agent or business manager?"

"My wife has an agent down in California," I told him. "Actually, he's a lawyer. He handles shit for her. I've never met him. Mike something."

He arched an eyebrow. "Mike Selig?"

"Could be. Some guy down there in Hollywood told her that she'd better have a Jew watching her back or she'd soon end up without a pot to piss in. So she got Mike."

Mark said, "You should get your wife to call Selig and see if he'll take you on as a client."

"How come?"

"Because you need fucking *representation*, Red. You can't negotiate for yourself. We just don't do things that way."

Ultimately, I accepted an offer from ESPN. I would join Con Horwitz in the broadcast booth early in October. Later on, when I had to have dinner, and spend three hours in the booth, with Horwitz, I decided that I was the most underpaid guy I knew.

As he stood and prepared to leave, Mark Richardson said, "I don't think you'll need to work with a voice coach. You speak with a very prominent Canadian accent that will lend an international flavor to our broadcasts."

Sheri sounded delighted when I told her about my new job. "You'll love working with adults instead of overgrown children," she said. "Weren't you flattered that the boss flew in just to see you? Usually they just send one of their flunkies."

"He's just another suit to me," I said. "If he fucks up, they'll just replace him with another suit and I'm not sure anyone will be able to tell the difference."

FOUR

L.T. Briggs threatened me with death blows to the brain if I didn't stop by Northup University before I flew down to California to shack up with Sheri.

He wanted me to be there for Northup's home opener against the University of Alberta Dinosaurs, the only team in the Western Canadian Conference with a worse record than Northup over the past couple of decades.

A week had passed. The doctor had run a dozen tests, told me not to get any more concussions and discharged me from the hospital.

The cobwebs in my head had pretty much cleared up by then, and I felt better than OK except that I felt plenty of anxiety over the sudden upheaval in my life. I swallowed my last couple of Tylenol 3s, wandered out of Bayporte General Hospital and took and took a taxi home.

My own living room looked unfamiliar to me. Flash had flown to New York City to look at some apartments. I would have welcomed his company and dreaded the day, which would probably arrive soon, when, out of restlessness, he moved out again.

After showering, shaving and dressing presentably, I got into my own car, pointed it in the direction of the U. and, within minutes, sat marveling at how, in my rearview mirror, the skyline of Bayporte sprang up before me like a handful of erections. My home and native city, like a half-dozen of its American sisters, seemed in a hurry to get as big and fat as possible.

Certain cities were unique: Boston, New York, San Francisco, Los Angeles (sometimes), Montreal,

Washington, D.C. But the others, and I had spent time investigating virtually all of them, had started to resemble each other far too much. I put that out of my mind and thought about nothing in particular as I pulled into the Northup University parking lot.

"You got knocked cold last week, huh? That'll show my boys what a *real* man can endure," L.T. said as we sat in his office in Northup Stadium on Friday afternoon, the day before the Alberta game.

L.T.'s office had a huge window that looked onto my old stadium. His office had been decorated, not altogether unstylishly, in brown and gold, Northup University's fighting colors. On his wall hung several inspirational messages aimed at those college athletes who, through some happy accident, had learned to read:

THERE IS NO 'I' IN TEAM
IF YOU SEE A FUMBLE, PICK IT UP!
PRETTY GIRLS DON'T PUT OUT FOR LOSERS

"Does the chancellor know about those pearls of wisdom?" I asked L.T.

"He's on our side. Thinks the messages might work."

L.T. probably had a point. Dr. Grant Miller, Northup's chancellor, smiled often, shook hands with everyone and wore a Northup tie to work every day. He seemed to think that his job consisted solely and wholly of beating the millionaire (and occasionally billionaire) bushes for heavy money. He also seemed to think L.T.'s job was to win football games, period. Dr. Miller, like most other university bosses, surely had been told by his rich alumni that he could extract more endowment by winning football games than merely by smiling, shaking hands and brownnosing at rubber-chicken dinners.

"Before the game," L.T. was saying, "I want to introduce you to my players. I want you to give them a little inspirational talk. Something that'll make their hearts and brains speed up a bit."

"What do you want me to say?"

"Oh, just tell them one of those dumb-ass pep talks you've heard over the years," he said.

"Such as?"

"Shit, man, I don't know. Tell them about how you played an entire game against Alberta with a sprained thigh and a bruise on your left testicle."

L.T. also insisted that I attend a reception in the Alumni Lounge following the game. I'd have fun, he said, and meet some nice folks. Some of my ex-teammates would be there, a few of whom had gone from being Northup University greats who had progressed from Honorable Mention to First Team All-Canadian in the three decades that had passed since they played football.

"Scoliosis will be there," L.T. said. "I want you to get a good look at him."

"Who?"

"Scoliosis Robinson."

"That can't be his real name," I said, laughing.

L.T. glowered at me. "Listen to me, Red. Scoliosis Robinson can win us some football games if we can get him."

Scoliosis Robinson, according to L.T., lived in the tiny town of Merde, Louisiana. An ebony spectacle, he stood six-three and weighed two-forty. He was so big, fast and powerful that most opponents were afraid to tackle him.

"Sounds like a stud," I said. "He has decent grades, right?"

L.T.'s face went red. He swallowed hard as he pulled open a desk drawer and pulled out a document.

"This is a confidential thing," he said, pushing the document across the desk to me. "I'd hate to think what the English professors here would say if they saw it."

I held the document but looked at L.T.'s worried face as he continued.

"There's a rule that says a high school student has to fill out that form in the presence of the head coach. In my office this morning, I asked Scoliosis to fill it out. He said he wanted to take it home, fill it out there and mail it to me. I said, 'No, guy, you have to do it here. It's not hard. You just have to fill in your name here and your address there. Put down your mum and dad's names and your high school.' When he got to where he had to write down his sport of choice, he looked up at me and said, 'What's this mean?' I said, 'Your favorite sport is football, isn't it? That's why you're here.' He nodded, so I said, 'Just write *football*, guy.' Only he didn't write that. Look at what he wrote."

Scoliosis Robinson had written "*boobies*."

"Boobies?" I glanced up at L.T.

"Can you fuckin' believe it?"

"Boobies," I repeated. "He didn't misspell the word by that much. At least he got the first letter right. I've seen worse."

"Gimme that back," L.T. said, snatching away the document. He stuffed the paper back inside his drawer and slammed it shut.

"Boobies," I said again, chuckling.

"He can do us a ton of good, Red," L.T., his lips thin and eyes narrow. "If we get Scoliosis Robinson wearing that Northup brown and gold, we're gonna do some serious damage to those other teams."

...

I had agreed to meet up with Lord Larry and Lady Joy that evening for cocktails at Placid Oaks Country Club, but that was OK. They could be more entertaining than booze. Long ago, they had established themselves as the most pretentious people in Canadian history.

Placid Oaks had a tacit whites-only policy, which was fine with the many rich Asians who resided in Bayporte because they didn't want to join anyway. When I arrived, I walked into the dining room and saw a sea of old white faces who stared at each other or stared at me because I was a young man walking like an old one.

"Here's to Mother Earth and all she's given us," Lord Larry said as he fired up a cigar. Placid Oaks, like everywhere else, prohibited smoking indoors; but who was going to tell Lord Larry to put it out?

"I had to remind my people today that we're in the business of finding diamonds, gold and silver, not tons of dirt!" Lord Larry told us.

Then, "You know where to find diamonds, gold and silver, don't you, Red? And don't be a bloody smartmouth and say, 'You find those things in a jewelry store'!"

"Tell me," I said.

"You find them under the ground, mostly. Centuries ago, when the Natives owned this continent, they found fist-sized chunks of gold lining the rivers, but they had no use for the stuff. Too bad for them, eh?"

"How's business these days?' I asked, to be polite.

"Never as good as it could be," he said with a sigh. "I mine precious metals, yes, but I drill for oil, too, and that's when I have to deal with the Arabs who jack around with the oil and petroleum prices the way most guys jack around with their dicks. I've said to the sheikhs' faces, 'You guys should stop worrying about OPEC shit and start worrying about becoming better Muslims. We'd all be better off for it.'"

Lord Larry and Lady Joy were a physically handsome couple. He was tall and thin, with abundant gray hair and a year-round suntan. He wore Savile Row suits and Bally shoes. Lady Joy, the consummate society lady, had dirty blonde hair and flew down to Los Angeles to get the finest available boob jobs, butt tucks and facelifts. Around her neck and wrists she wore some of the best rocks her husband had ever dug up.

"What's Sheri up to?" Lord Larry wanted to know. They repeated how proud they were that Sheri, their daughter, had married me. "Got any problems we can fix? I know the prime minister. He owes me one or two."

"We're getting along OK. She's down there and I'm up here," I said.

"I think it's the strangest thing," Lady Joy said, shaking her head. "Why does Sheri want to be another Hollywood actor?"

I said I didn't know. As a retired athlete, I had met many people, washed-up jocks, who went the Hollywood route. They all ended up miserable.

If they got lucky, they had the directors and editors who could make them look good. They could make the radio and TV talk-show rounds and come across as clever, even charismatic, and they could be downright charming at special events. But they were never themselves, because they didn't have a "self." Something vital was missing from them; what was left was a maniac who distrusted everyone who failed to tell them how wonderful they were; to such maniacs, fame and money were the only meaningful things in life. I had sat in movie theaters for years watching them, marveling at their talent, laughing and crying with them. But I had never wanted to have any of them as a personal friend, I believed the sordid things I read about them in the gossip rags.

Sheri had done the TV pilot because half a dozen ABC movers and shakers persuaded her to do so. They had been after her to try starring in a series since they saw her in commercials.

"She decided to do it," I told her mum and dad, "after her agent gave her a project to look over. Her character would be the star, and that character would be very much like Sheri herself—cracking wise, talking back, but very beautiful and surrounded by friends and admirers."

Lady Joy closed her eyes and shuddered. "A Hollywood actress."

"Who watches TV, anyway?" Lord Larry asked. "I mean, people watch news and sports, but what about the other stuff? Whenever I've watched at night, all I saw was a bunch of sissy boys showing off and laughing at themselves. Is Sheri going to play a fag hag or something?"

"I hope not," I said. "So far, all she's doing is a pilot, which is just the first episode. They take that pilot to Las Vegas and show it at the convention. If a network likes it, they buy it and order more episodes. Sound OK?"

"I just don't want my daughter on TV being a fag hag, goofing around with sissy boys," said Lord Larry.

Sheri's show, called *Lally's Place,* featured Sheri as Lally, an HIV-positive cutie who ran a dodgy hotel in downtown Los Angeles.

"Why," I asked her, "does your character have to be infected with HIV?"

"Because," she replied, "the producers think the audience will have more empathy for her. She's beautiful, smart, funny and tragic. Who can resist?"

I said to the Rawsons, "Lally is a kind of superwoman. She runs the hotel and her guests are all kinds of shady characters. They sass her and she sasses them back."

"I hope one of them is a doctor who can cure her HIV," Lord Larry said.

"I don't think Lally ever gets full-blown AIDS if the show becomes a hit," I said. "Of course, she'll have good days and bad days."

"What kind of name is Lally?" Lady Joy asked. "I've never heard of it."

"I guess the producers went online to find a different kind of name and that's what they got," I said.

"And why does it have to be a bad hotel in the wrong part of town?" Lady Joy asked.

"Maybe the producers thought poor people were funnier than normal people," Lord Larry said. "I'm assuming it's meant to be funny. Is it?"

I shrugged. "Not from the scripts Sheri has told me about. But maybe it will be a big hit anyway. They've sure dumbed it down enough."

"How's Sheri doing with it? Can she act?" Lord Larry asked me.

"Doing her best, I guess. She says her lines are so retarded that she feels like making cretinous faces when she delivers them. Anyway, the inability to act has rarely held back any performer from attaining TV fame."

"When's it going to be on TV?" he asked.

"It has a chance to go on in late October or late January. In October, the networks look at which rats' nests people are watching and which rats' nests viewers aren't watching. They do that in January, too. The rats' nests nobody watches get cancelled and replaced with better rats' nests."

Lord Larry said, "I've never seen any rats' nests. All I've seen are sissy boys goofing around."

I nodded. "Those are the successful shows. The actors' names and faces change."

"But they're still sissy boys goofing around."

"Which network?" Lord Larry asked.

"ABC," I said.

"Which one's ABC?"

"Al Michaels and John Madden. Ted Koppel, Peter Jennings years ago."

Lord Larry frowned. "Still don't know it."

"The networks are hard to tell apart sometimes. ABC is big when it comes to sports like the Olympics."

"The Olympics," Lord Larry said. "Bunch of sissy boys. You see how they dress? They keep pulling their underwear out of their ass cracks. And the women, they look like men. Didn't see one decent pair of titties on any of them."

"ABC," I said, "is often in last place in the

ratings."

"Yeah? Good." Lord Larry took a sip of his cocktail.

We got to talking about Northup University and its nonstop need for money to build a winning football team. Lord Larry, a Northup alumnus who had stayed in Bayporte and made piles of money, bought the U. overhead lights for night football games, a playing surface for the stadium and three quarterbacks who were skilled at throwing interceptions and being sacked. He'd also bought the school more brown and gold paint than it could ever use.

Lord Larry said, "All I want in return for my kindness—"

"Is to have the best college football team in Canada," I interrupted.

"Bloody right."

"They were smart to bring on L.T. Briggs as our new head coach," I said.

"Well, that's a good start. But you don't win football games with a bunch of wimps and pussies. He's going to have to do some very aggressive recruiting."

"What do you mean?" I asked.

"Get the best talent out there. Don't do anything illegal, but bend the rules a bit."

"Have you heard about Scoliosis Robinson?"

Lord Larry nodded. "He is the consummate football player. He can make it to the end zone just as fast as a Paki runs towards the smell of curry."

"That fast, eh?"

Lord Larry lit up another cigar. A few people at another table glowered at him, but he paid them no mind. If they didn't like his smoking, that was *their* problem.

"L.T.'s concerned that we won't be able to outbid some other schools for Scoliosis," Lord Larry said. "They'll give him the usual goodies—a car, a condo, a 'bikini inspector' job that'll pay him more than two gynecologists make. I said, 'I've got an idea. Let's give that spade his own convenience store. Let him stock it with crack and meth if he wants to!'"

Lady Joy admonished Lord Larry with a now-now narrowing of her eyes and a little tap on his sleeve.

Sheri, Flash and I had always been unable to shut up that old guy. He had been talking trash for as long as I could remember.

As children, we all called each other names because we didn't know any better. But if you have half an ounce of sense in your head, as you get older you start to appreciate just how offensive that kind of talk can be. As an adult, I've come to understand that colored people know that nobody can shut up someone like Lord Larry, who has zillions of dollars.

I stretched out a bit and grimaced. "Sorry, folks," I said to Lord Larry and Lady Joy, "but I'm starting to go brain-dead. I think I better go home." What I really wanted to do was be by myself and get shitfaced.

I went home and thought of L.T. Briggs, who was even less tolerant than Lord Larry, that soul, and what I would say to his players the following day so they could beat the Alberta Dinosaurs.

FIVE

Blown-up images of Dino the pet dinosaur from The *Flintstones* covered the walls of the Northup dressing room. Only thing was, those images had been crossed out with a red marker.

"Nice touch," I said to L.T. as we stood drinking coffee in a corner and watched our players struggle into their equipment.

"We put up those pictures to remind our boys of who the enemy is," he said. "I knew it would be a terrific way to make our fans hate that bitch and her team."

"'Bitch?'"

"Yeah! Fuck that whore and everyone who looks like her!"

L.T. spun around to face his players.

"Fuck Alberta! Fuck every zit on her ugly face!"

L.T. was getting his boys pumped up for action. A couple of players took his bait.

"Alberta sucks cock!" someone yelled.

"She sucks big hairy cocks!" hollered someone else.

I frowned and sipped coffee. "L.T., what do blow jobs have to with Alberta?"

"She's a broad, right? Broads suck cock, don't they?"

I shrugged.

"Who sucks cock?" L.T. yelled at his men.

"Alberta!"

"How?"

"With her mouth!" everyone shouted back.

I drained my coffee cup and said, "L.T., do you

understand that Alberta isn't a woman, it's the name of the province that the University of Alberta is located in? The province is named for some English royalty who died years ago. You know that, don't you?"

"Can't *you* see," L.T. retorted, "that I'm gettin' 'em all worked up?"

Outside, I met L.T.'s three assistants, all of whom wore royal blue sports shirts, khaki slacks. I smiled up at the late-September sky, always grateful for good weather. I also enjoyed being back here at the stadium where I had enjoyed so much success and adoration. As I gazed at the crowd that filled less than half of the 40,000-seat facility, Homer Michaels, the Kodiaks' offensive coordinator, approached me.

"Your boys ready to make these fans happy today?" I asked him.

"Hope so." Homer kept his eyes on a pretty cheerleader who wore the Northup dark-brown tank top and gold pleated skirt. She had blonde hair, a tan and long, slender legs. "You've met your share of world-class pussy in your travels, eh?"

"I guess." Then, "We got a good quarterback right now, don't we?"

"Does his best."

"Who's that girl?' I asked him as we both stared at the cheerleader.

"Her name's Candy." He licked his lips. "I know I'm old enough to be her father, but I'd bang her silly if I got the chance."

Presently I met Jeff Redding, the defensive coordinator.

"We ready to show 'em who's boss?" I asked him.

"She's the boss," he said, pointing at Candy, who

was deep in conversation with her colleagues.

I nodded. "She's a cutie."

"For sure. But I guess she doesn't compare to some of the poontang you had when you were with the Invaders, going city to city and boffing all those NFL groupies."

The last coach I met was Colin Rinaldo, head of the defensive secondary.

"Looks like we have some quality talent out there in the secondary," I said to him.

"The only quality talent I'm interested in right now is over there," he said, pointing at Candy. "She can be my wide receiver or tight end. Whatever she wants."

Soon both teams returned to their dressing rooms for a few last-minute words from the coaches and anxious trips to the washroom before the game began. L.T. ordered his boys to sit down and shut up, then he introduced me.

His introduction flattered me. I was a true Bayporter, a distinguished alumnus and eternal Kodiak who once, nearly all by himself, had beaten the University of Toronto despite having multiple serious injuries.

L.T. put a brotherly arm around my shoulders and said to the Kodiaks, "If Red, banged up as he is right now, knew that we needed him, he'd suit up and get out there, and he'd win it for us!"

I had little idea of what to say to them until I looked around the room and saw the prairie boys' doughy faces and the city kids' wary eyes. I saw the big white numbers on their dark-brown jerseys, the same kind I had worn years earlier. It made me realize that we *did* have something of significance in common.

Northup, like most other Canadian universities, lacked the resources to recruit the top American athletes, so they made do with homegrown talent.

I started out by telling this roomful of Kodiaks that they were very fortunate to have the privilege of playing for a stand-up guy like L.T. Briggs and his staff.

Out of fear of boring my audience shitless, I said the next thing that popped into my mind, which was this:

"Gentlemen, just a minute or two ago I was outside and I saw something that reminded me of a long-ago game against the Dinosaurs. There's a cheerleader out there, a pretty blonde named Candy. Do you know her?"

Several players nodded and muttered, as if they had screwed her in the past week. Which they probably had.

I nodded back and continued.

"Well, gentlemen, not so long ago, Northup had a cheerleader named Darcie who looked enough like Candy to be her sister—and in fact she *was* Candy's sister. To make a long, sad story short, the Dinosaurs came to town, just like today, and on the night before the big game, a bunch of them got drunk and started looking for trouble here on campus. Darcie was just crossing the street on her way to her sorority house when the Dinosaurs spotted her. She tried to run but they caught up with her, and I don't even want to think about what they did to our poor Darcie. So when you're out there today and Candy's cheering for you, just remember Darcie and what those Dinosaurs did to her."

L.T. Briggs yelled, "Let's go get those bastards!"

The Kodiaks bounded out of the locker rooms like, well, bears; they hollered, pounded the walls and slammed their fists into the lockers. They hungered for the flesh of the Dinosaurs.

L.T. pumped my hand and smiled. "Thanks for that, Red. Was it all bullshit?"

I shrugged. "Most of it."

"Which part was true?" he asked.

"Well, there *was* a Northup cheerleader named Darcie."

"Did she do anything special?"

"Sure did," I said. "She gave Flash Gortton gonorrhea."

At halftime, Alberta led by a score of 12-4.

Neither team scored a touchdown. The Dinosaurs got within two yards of the end zone on four occasions and each time had to settle for a field goal. On two of those attempts, the Alberta kicker would have missed, but a Northup player, trying to block the kick, inadvertently corrected the ball's path and it went through the uprights. Northup got its four points from safeties by touching the Dinosaurs' quarterback as he slipped in his own end zone.

In the locker room, L.T. was beside himself with rage.

"I hate that score!" He scowled at his players. "But what *really* busts my onions is how the bunch of you sleepwalked through those first two quarters. What the fuck? Did someone put dope in the Gatorade?

"You boys showed no initiative, no motivation.

I'm personally going to take responsibility for the way you just stood around with your fingers up your asses those first two quarters. I don't think it's a matter of lacking courage. I think it's about no aggression. I think all of you left your killer instincts in that Lambda Cum Fuck sorority house.

"Girls and football don't go together," he told them. "I'll bet every one of you shot a load or two into some wet pussy last night, and if you deny it I'll call you a liar right to your face." He took a deep breath and added, "Well, this game today is a loser, but starting tomorrow, there's gonna be a lot less sorority sisters being sexually serviced on Saturday night by the football players in this room.

"The key to having a winning football team on Sunday afternoon can be summed up in two words: jerking off. When I was a young punk they told me jerking off was a bad thing, but we've since learned different. The player who waxes his own dolphin the night before has plenty of focus and aggression for the big day. Beating your own meat has been the secret to any number of football teams that went out there and won a big game!

"You 'men' acted like little boys out there during the first half today. Made fools of yourselves, me and Red Crossley, a great Canadian footballer, plus many of your mums and dads, too. If you had jerked off last night, you would have been ready to kick some ass today, and next Saturday night you're gonna do just that. Next week the Northup University Kodiaks will ready to play some serious football, and you can write that down and put it on the Internet for the whole fuckin' world to read!"

The Kodiaks took care of business during the

second half. Pete Sonnenberg threw two touchdown passes—they were both inadvertently aimed at Alberta players and batted around by both teams but ended up in the arms of Northup receivers. The Kodiaks won the game, and a couple of linebackers hoisted L.T. onto their shoulders and carried him off the field. I wondered just how many fans or press photographers noticed the masturbatory way L.T. pumped his fists in victory, or what it meant. But then, who cared?

I met Scoliosis Robinson, and all I could think was, *Wow*.

Everybody kept a respectful distance from him in the lounge after the game. In his gold satin warmup suit and Versace sunglasses, he looked like a comfortable cross between Jamie Foxx and Jim Brown. His chest, arms and legs were massive—even, as the kids liked to say, *awesome*. Of course, I hadn't seen him play yet, and maybe he was really more show than substance. If so, it wouldn't be the first time that a high school stud simply couldn't cut it on the college playing field. But then, none of those failed athletes looked half as ready for action as Scoliosis Robinson did.

I took L.T. aside and said, "Coach, isn't there a rule against a Western Canadian college bringing in a high school athlete for a campus visit *before* the athlete has graduated?"

L.T. told me, as if explaining to a small child that we do *not* make poo-poo in our pants, "We'll just keep it our little secret."

Scoliosis stood next to his brother, Rickey, a handsome, smiling man in his mid-20s. Like Scoliosis, Rickey was tall and muscular, but, side by side, Scoliosis made Rickey look wimpy. Rickey wore a Bill Blass dark-gray suit with a paisley silk tie, and he carried a briefcase. Clearly, he had come here as his brother's agent, business advisor and confidant.

A high school sports star who already had an agent was a common thing. The boys with remarkable athletic ability, the ones who actually had shots at going pro, often had representation, and cars, before they were old enough to drive. Universities wanted to win football games; dads wanted to get the best deals for their athletically gifted sons. Still, the sight of it— teenaged males having sports scholarships, cars, money and girls—sometimes freaked me out.

When, years earlier, Flash and I had signed on to become Kodiaks, my Uncle Rex had been our agent and Lord Larry Rawson served as our financial advisor. We liked to tell people that we should have held out for a better deal. Flash and I got a sports car apiece—a Camaro and a Corvette; I can't remember who got which—and Uncle Rex scored four tickets to every Northup home game. Lord Larry paid Flash and me great money to stand around and look important at one of his mining sites during the next four summers.

The cars and cushy jobs were modest compensation for Flash and me, two Bayporte boys who would go on to become All-Canadian college players and put plenty of bums in the stadium seats. But we were going to stay home attend Northup University regardless of those inducements. Sheri

Rawson, the love of our lives, had decided to enroll at Northup even though she could have gone to any American or European college. She wanted to piss off her mother, I suspected. Lady Joy, that most charming of snobs, wanted to send Sheri to Wellesley, Smith, Barnard or Heidelberg, where they would make a proper lady of the girl.

"Mum," Sheri had said, "I already know how to chew with my mouth closed."

Flash and I were quite happy to stay in our native city and get our education at Northup. We'd have happily stayed in college forever and never gone out into the cold, cruel world.

Before chasing after Scoliosis Robinson, L.T. had gone to much trouble to make a Kodiak of leopard-fast DeShonn Jones, a wide receiver from some obscure high school in Arkansas. Two dozen colleges wanted him, but L.T., determined to have DeShonn and Scoliosis, flew to the States and drove a rental car to DeShonn's lean-to that sheltered the boy's parents, uncle, many siblings and a few cats and dogs.

On his visit, L.T. sat with the family and watched game shows on daytime TV. He had a baby on each knee and tried to keep his legs together so that the dogs couldn't sniff his balls.

"That little house in the middle of nowhere," he said later, "smelled like they'd just held a five-day farting contest in there without bothering to air it out."

DeShonn, his family said, was not home right then, but they expected him at any moment. So L.T. sat there. For the next several hours, he held the babies on his knee, tried to keep the dogs' noses away from his crotch and did his very best not to breathe through his nose.

DeShonn stepped in, said, "Coach, I'll be right back. Gotta take care of somethin," and stepped back out. L.T. struggled over to the window and watched DeShonn zoom off in a white Mercedes with a Washington state license plate and an assistant coach in the passenger's seat.

Flying back to Bayporte that evening, L.T. wished he hadn't been such a gentleman during his visit with the Jones family. "I should've punched those fuckin' dogs in the nose."

Coaches and faculty members always rationalize their recruitment violations as a necessary evil.

Everyone does it, they argue, and it's a good way for the smaller, poorer schools to compete against the bigger, richer institutions. Getting the best possible players for your team is difficult enough; keeping them in good standing is often even harder. I'd heard about an entire Rose Bowl team that had received A's and B's in a "media studies" course they had never even heard of.

The fact is, every college team that has won consistently over a number of years has cheated, at least in minor ways. But really, what's so awful about giving some kid a scholarship, keeping his pockets full with income from a cushy job and making sure that his professors give him better than decent grades? College football can rescue some kids from a life of stealing cars and slanging rocks.

A big business, college ball has provided money for more library wings and professors' salaries than most people will ever realize. Endowment from athletics has bought many computers so that pencil-necked, geeky business majors could hack into my bank accounts and complicate my life.

If a kid can get a free trip through college by playing music or writing provocative essays, why can't kids get that same education by putting 50,000 bums into stadium seats?

Of course, nobody had to tell any of that to L.T., Scoliosis or Rickey. They understood what was going on. The four of us stood in a private conversation in the Alumni Lounge at Northup University as people staggered about.

"Here's the deal," said Rickey. "We have offers. I'm not saying who, but plenty of schools out there want my bro and are willing to pay thousands to get him to suit up for them. If he went to an American school, he would win the Heisman Trophy in his first year."

"If he went to Northup," L.T. said, "he would be in the starting lineup in his first year, if that's what he wanted. He could be the boss and call the plays."

Rickey shook his head. "He don't want to be the boss. He just wants to play football." He added, "Don't be worried about his character, either. If he signs a letter of intent with you, he'll be here on time and in shape."

I asked Scoliosis if he was concerned about injuries during his final year in high school football.

"An injury could cost you lots of money," I said, grinning.

"Scoliosis won't get hurt," said Rickey. "He'll be the one *causing* the hurt."

L.T. patted Scoliosis' shoulder and beamed at him. "You'll be the best we've ever had."

I tried not to be insulted by that remark.

After a moment, I tried again to get Scoliosis to

speak. I had never actually heard him say anything and wanted some sort of assurance that he wasn't mute. I wanted to look into his eyes, just to make sure his pupils were normal and he wasn't high or anything, but all I saw were the opaque lenses of sunglasses that probably cost more than most students' books and tuition.

Scoliosis said, "You want to know if I am concerned about gettin hurt this year. No, I am not worried about that. Worryin would make me feel anxietied."

Rickey told us an anecdote about when he and Scoliosis were little kids, the point, I guess, was to make us appreciate what a colorful little bugger Scoliosis had been.

One evening, the two kids had gone to the movies with their father. Scoliosis wasn't much older than a kindergartener at that time. They had gone to see a double bill, *Magnum Force* and *Dirty Harry.*

"Little kids always crack me up," Rickey said, grinning. "As soon as we got back home, Scoliosis said, 'Daddy, if I had a gun I'd blow your head clean off.'"

"What's up with his name?" I asked. "Did your parents really name him Scoliosis?"

Rickey laughed. "He was named for our uncle, Scolomore, but nobody could pronounce it, so we started calling him Scoliosis. It's easier for everyone to say."

At the end of our conversation, L.T. told Scoliosis to have fun in high school and not to make any big decisions about college until he'd checked out everything with the Kodiaks.

"What number do you want on your Northup

jersey?" L.T. asked Scoliosis.

"No number," I said. "Just a big dollar sign."

"Yeah, baby!" Rickey blurted, offering me a high five.

SIX

After helping L.T. in his recruiting efforts, I met up with my old friend Phil Ruble and checked out some of Bayporte's ladies. I drove out to Pandora's Box, a strip joint in a vast shopping mall on the eastern edge of town. I couldn't find a parking space anywhere near the strip joint, so I parked at the other end. A few doors down from Pandora's Box, another strip joint, Good Girls, advertised as its headliner this way:

This week
SUZY BOOBIES
38-24-36
Natural and Delicious

Phil Ruble sat waiting for me at Pandora's bar, a place practically bursting with single men on the prowl. Rising young brownnosers in pinstriped suits sat talking business with STD-infected females aged 19 to 50.

I said hey to Phil, who gave me a little nod and continued talking to the spacy, gum-chewing, hair-twisting blonde standing next to him.

"Let's go sit," I told him.

He nodded and we ordered four Canadian Comforts over ice, then took our drinks over to a booth.

"That story about the Kodiaks over the Dinos? I can't believe how fast you wrote it," I said.

He shrugged. "Easy job. I just wrote about how good the Kodiaks looked and how bad the other team looked. It wasn't worth reading."

Phil, the editor and main scribe at *Canadian Sports Online*, had been my friend—or at least one of my more likable acquaintances—since my years as a football stud at Northup. Phil was such a decent human being that I wondered how he had managed to stay in journalism for so long.

"I saw you down on the field before the game," he said. "How come you didn't come up to the press box and say hello?"

"I figured you were too busy. How's your arthritis?"

"Worse every day. I hope you die before you get old, Red."

Phil, nearly fifty, a veteran of two wives and countless girlfriends, had resigned himself mostly to porn videos and jerking off.

"Just as well," he said. "Reporters shouldn't be married. We're too devoted to our jobs, and we get so mad when we turn in flawless copy and some idiotic editor or typesetter goofs it up and our beautiful work ends up with a typo or two in it. This is journalism; it's not like we're writing the Great Canadian Novel. We go home at night, exhausted and unable to share ourselves with anyone. It takes a fool to marry one of us. If a woman is foolish enough to marry us, she deserves what she gets."

An argument started over by the pool tables, then died down. Pandora's Box was almost too loud for conversation.

"Why do you come here?" I asked.

"I come here to have fun and meet interesting people," Phil said.

A server struggled through the crowd to deliver four more glasses of Canadian Comfort over ice.

"We'll be joined soon by a couple of my little honeys," Phil told me. "You OK with that?"

I nodded. "Just don't ask me to boff them."

He shook his head. "No, they're for me. Not sure if I can rise to the occasion, though. You know what I'm looking forward to, Red? Old age. That way, I can just let them do all the work."

"You said a minute ago that you hoped I died before I got old. Anyway, you're probably the first person who's ever looked forward to old age," I said.

Phil rubbed his face. "Maybe I'll grow a mustache and beard. I think I read in *Playboy* that face fuzz helps in cunnilingus."

I asked him about sports. On the banquet circuit, if I decided to do that again, they always wanted to hear some tasty, nasty observations, and Phil could be a good source. Plus, he wouldn't get mad if I repeated them at the lectern.

After a couple of decades of covering sports, Phil, uninterested in political correctness or diplomacy, had acquired some biases. Now, with plenty of Canadian Comfort in his bloodstream, he shared with me his many and diverse pet peeves.

"Ice hockey? The NHL? What is that?" He drained his drink and started on the next one. "A bunch of Canadian, eastern Europeans and Russians who fight for control of a disc made of vulcanized rubber so that they can shoot it into a net. What a fuckin' joke! Want to make it better, just suspend the rules. Nobody has to wear a helmet and every player can hit his opponent with his stick as hard as he wants and as often as he wants. Do you remember when Sidney Crosby took a puck in the mouth and lost some teeth? He had a fractured jaw, too, and that was one of the most exciting moments in hockey that year. Or when some player gets hit with a stick and half of his teeth go flying onto the ice? The trainer has to take him into the dressing room to do some oral surgery. The player guzzles down a couple of high-protein shakes and gets back out on the ice. That's what the fans want to see. They also want to see some player get knocked cold on the ice so that he has to be carried off. It's even better if the guy's head cracks and there's brain matter on the ice. The Zamboni can come in later and clean it all up."

"What about Major League Baseball?"

Phil scowled. "What about it? They want to suspend Alex Rodriguez for doing something that's made him a much better player. Steroids? Look at Roger Clemens, Barry Bonds, Jose Canseco. They were all juicers, and because of it, baseball has been far more exciting. Let them stick needles into their butts if it will give them that extra edge. Don't suspend A-Rod because he used steroids; just let him do his thing and post those amazing numbers. Also, induct Pete Rose into the Hall of Fame despite his gambling activities. Worse things have been done by better men. Shit, if I had to play over a hundred and sixty games, I'd juice up, too."

"My Uncle Rex likes pro basketball."

"Gee, that's nice. I'm glad Bayporte doesn't have an NBA franchise. The game bores me. All those seven-foot freaks showing off their hairy armpits."

"You like boxing, though."

He nodded. "Boxing is two big boys beating the shit out of each other, and it doesn't pretend to be anything more than that. Also, I love watching all that violence. It's very cathartic for me."

"Flash is writing about sports and whatnot," I said. "He's moved to New York."

"I know. He emails me now and then. I think *Playboy* wants his football piece."

"You know more about his activities than I do, Phil."

Phil smiled. "Oh, he says he'll catch up with you in Bayporte or Los Angeles. He called me when he was here signing his books downtown. We went out and got pissed. I think he got laid—I *know* he did, because she wouldn't give up. She's one of the lovelies who will be by soon."

"Phil, talk to me. Have you got a freak scene lined up for us tonight?"

He sat back. "No, don't worry. The four of us can just hang out and see what comes up."

Then he half-rose and waved his arms at someone behind me. His two girlfriends.

The ladies slid in with us, Suzy Boobies alongside me and her friend Trisha got cozy with Phil. When moving aside to give Suzy some room, I accidentally poked one of her boobies with my elbow.

"Mmm, that was nice," she said.

Ecdysiasts, most of the time, turned me on very little, but I did respect them as artists. Also, they were different, well out of the mainstream, and therefore fun for conversation.

By two-thirty in the morning, we had taken our little party to Good Girls, an establishment where they believed that the two-o'clock closing time bylaw did not apply to them.

Phil and I stared at our drinks, wondering how many more we could swallow before one or both of us barfed. Suzy and Trisha sat with us at the bar.

Phil had fallen into an alcoholic funk, rambling about how his woman had left him and nobody seemed to have much use for him any longer. Trisha, a nineteen-year-old lush, drank shots of vodka and kept ordering more.

Suzy Boobies, a natural 38, had a Goth look: black hair, plenty of mascara and black lipstick. Black sweater and matching jeans, too. Crow's feet and plenty or wrinkles around her mouth. I guessed her age at between over 39 and Way Too Old for Sex Work.

"I strip for God," she told me. "I read from the New Testament during my act and sit on the book as I masturbate."

"Is that the message you think your audience is getting?" I asked her.

"Yes, even if they don't know it. There are many ways to reach God, and some don't seem like ways even though they really are. Mine is one."

"You're sort of a preacher," I said.

"I *am* a preacher," she replied. "I was ordained online by the Church of Eternal Deliverance. I can marry and bury people."

"Do you fuck people you meet as a stripper?"

"I never use profanity. I find it offensive."

"So sorry," I said.

"I'm thirsty!" she said to the bartender. "How about a double Canadian Comfort?"

The bartender served her the drink, and she knocked it back in one swallow.

Suzy pressed her magnificent mammaries against my arm and rubbed her knee against mine.

"Small audience tonight," she said. "When there

are more people, I do a longer show. I insist on stripping to gospel music. It makes people take my act more seriously."

"I believe you've met my pal Flash Gortton," I said.

"I certainly have."

"He is a beautiful soul."

Suzy smirked. "The rest of him is cute, too." Then, "My boyfriend in Vancouver says that when I perform, he can just *feel* something beautiful and divine happening in the room, like God is watching."

Phil eased himself off his barstool and put his arm around Trisha.

"Gotta go, Red," he said. "I've had far too many drinks and smokes tonight. You have my contact info and I have yours. We'll touch base again soon."

Phil and Trisha left the bar clinging to each other like two lushes needing physical support. I turned to Suzy, grabbed her hand and gave it a quick peck.

"Suzy, I know you're a woman of the cloth, so I hate to tell you this, but I'm an atheist."

She shook her head. "No. There's no such thing, Atheists believe in God. They're just mad at Him because of all the bad things that have happened to them."

"Well, anyway, I'm also married, and I have a flight later on this morning."

Suzy Boobies nodded. "Marriage is a good thing for a man. Most of the men I know are happily married, including my boyfriend."

She reached down and gave my fly a long, loud scratch.

"I've enjoyed our visit, Suzy," I told her. "You've helped take away my worries for a few hours. Maybe there *is* something to your God-stuff."

"Red," she said, "let's take Communion."

"I told you, I don't go to church."

"No, dummy, let's do it *now*."

She took my hand and put it on her breast.

"Here is where you find God, Red."

"I'm not in the mood for this, Suzy," I told her.

"I can deal with your reluctance," she said, downing her drink. "I'm staying at a Best Western not far from the U. Pay the barkeep and let's go."

The people in my life have heard two versions of how my visit with Suzy ended. They have heard mine, which happened to be true, and Flash Gortton's decadent, sordid account of an evening that did not include him. Flash said that his version got a hell a lot more laughs than mine did.

Suzy's Best Western was fairly close to Northup University. I tailed her as she drove into the parking lot, said goodbye with a little honk and wave, then turned around and made the fairly brief drive back to my condo in downtown Bayporte. I took a couple of Tylenol 3s to ease the hangover that hadn't started, then crawled into my own bed, alone, and dropped off to sleep for a few hours.

Flash said that I, in a Canadian Comfort psychosis, had followed Suzy back to her Best Western, pulled in alongside her, threw her and her boobies over my shoulder and kicked in the door. I tore off all of our clothes and attached myself to her bed with her handcuffs as she mounted me and read from her Good Book as we became one in the Biblical sense.

I shook my head in disbelief at how my best friend could claim that I had engaged in such dastardly misdeeds. But I've always been one to let people think what they liked.

Later on, at Bayporte International Airport, I met up again with Flash, sort of. Chapters, a bookstore chain, had opened up a shop much bigger than it needed to be, and devoted a dump with two bins and a power wall to Flash's new book, *What to Do When Life's a B*tch*. A person just entering the store might have thought that *B*tch* was the only book Chapters had in stock.

I bought a copy to pretend to read during my flight to Los Angeles.

I smiled at the flight attendant as I settled into my seat and opened *B*tch*. That way, whichever boring person sat next to me knew better than to speak to me.

I nodded off and woke up just over our destination. *B*tch* lay in my lap, still completely unread. I would read it later. Or maybe I wouldn't. I felt sure that Flash had already said to me everything that was in his book.

The taxi ride from LAX to Westwood House gave me time to think about how millions of people could live in the same metropolitan area while refusing to make friends with each other.

"I can get you there fastuh," my hackie told me in his charming Haitian accent. "I know a shawt-cut."

His shortcut took us through countless side streets where crack dealers and other not-nice people glowered at us.

"The hotel is near UCLA," I told him. "We're too far east. Just keep driving towards the ocean and we'll probably make it to the hotel."

He flashed me a big white smile. "I gotcha, boss."

By and by we got there. I said nothing about how

had made $20 or $30 worth of wrong turns as I shoved my gold American Express card into his handheld reader, entered my personal identification number and when the screen said TIP, I punched in NO TIP.

I checked into Sheri's suite, took out my iPhone and called her. I got her answering message instead and told her that I had arrived and looked forward to screwing her brains out when she got in.

Within minutes my iPhone rang.

"You're here?" she asked. "Good."

"So, how's it goin', eh?"

"We are busy, busy, busy."

"Is that good or bad?" I asked.

"Mostly bad. We're doing a pilot that isn't funny. They're revising scripts, trying to keep what's funny and throw out the rest."

"You sound angry," I told her.

"Frustrated. This shouldn't be that difficult. Remember *Seinfeld*, *Friends*, *Three's Company*? There are a hundred other sitcoms that have worked. Just follow the formula and you've have a hit."

"For every hit sitcom," I reminded her, "there have been three dozen that were pure crap. A funny show that lasts a long time is the exception, not the rule."

"Are you trying to cheer me up or something?" Sheri said.

"Just telling you how it is, sweetness."

"Anyway, let's talk about dinner. Anami's at seven, OK?"

"Where is that?" I said.

"Flash flew in the other day. He's two floors below us. Ask him. He's been there lots of times."

I turned on the TV set and found a football game to listen to while I put away my things and checked out my room. The football game interested me very little but I paid attention to Con Horwitz as he covered the game. I knew I would be working with him soon.

"What a run!" Con exclaimed as a New York running back made a long gain in a meaningless game. "What an extraordinary athlete that man is!"

"Wait a minute, Con," said Abe Charles, the color man I would replace. "They're bringing it back. Holding."

"What a magnificent running back he has turned out to be! We've had Barry Sanders, Roger Craig, Emmit Smith and now—"

"Con, it doesn't fucking count!" I yelled at the TV. "Holding."

My iPhone rang.

"You watching the Giants?" Flash asked.

"Yeah, sort of. Con is getting on my nerves."

"Ted Charles is the head zebra down there. He's fixing the fucker as we speak. Come on down. We'll watch it together."

A couple of minutes later, I sat in Flash's room as we watched the Giants and Texans move the ball back and forth, with nobody scoring.

"That goddamn Ted Charles." Flash laughed. "He's been calling penalties and calling back touchdowns all day to make sure the Giants would win by enough."

"You think Charles has bet on the game?" I asked.

"I *know* he has, Red."

"How's your article coming along?" I asked. "Why are you here? I thought you were shopping for a place in New York."

He shrugged. "Best thing I've ever written. It's all about the NFL and its corruption. I'm here because I got restless and knew you two would be here. Thought I'd keep you company."

"Why do a smear piece on the NFL?"

"Because it's the right thing to do, and if I don't write it, it will go unwritten."

"Why don't you just leave it the fuck alone, Flash? What's football ever done to you besides make you rich and get you pussy?"

He arched an eyebrow. "Excuse me? I made football rich, and I got my own pussy. The game has gone downhill. It's too corporate and everyone's greedy. Where's the human element? The computers make the coaching decisions. The tickets are too expensive—it's supposed to be entertainment for the working man and his family." He shook his head and sighed. "Don't get me started. It'll all be in my article."

"Have you talked to Uncle Rex?"

Flash nodded. "He told me some stuff. He knows people. He hears things."

"Are you going to write about Ted Charles? I know he spends time in Bayporte during the off-season."

Flash grinned. "Ted keeps himself very busy with real estate. He financed some developments that sold very poorly and he lost a pile of money. You need money when you chase as much pussy as he does."

I scratched my head. "So he got out of debt and got money to spend on his girlfriends by betting on games—"

"Games he's worked. Then he makes damn sure

he calls two dozen penalties against the team he's bet against. Things turn out real nice for him that way." Then, "Ted gave someone a game. Someone we know."

"For real?" I asked, wide-eyed.

"No shit."

"Tell me who."

Flash smirked. "How was your flight from Bayporte?"

"Come on, don't jerk me around. Just tell me."

"Guess."

"Couldn't have been Uncle Rex. He wouldn't tell anyone if he had that kind of information."

"It wasn't Rex," Flash said, "and it wasn't Phil Ruble, either. Wrong gender."

I frowned. "A woman we both know, eh? Not Sheri."

"Think of an ordained minister we know."

I nearly fell off the sofa. *Suzy Boobies?*

"Bingo!"

"Suzy knows Ted Charles?"

Flash nodded. "She's one of his favorite squeezes."

"And he fixed a game for her?" I asked, shaking my head.

"He was happy to do it for her. She bet a bundle and won enough to buy a new car."

"Damn, I need a *drink*."

SEVEN

Most of the time, I try hard not to be a pain in anyone's ass, even when I'm in a restaurant where they have only two or three good things on their menu and my server tells me they're all out.

But, on that evening, I copped an attitude.

Damian, our server at Anami's in Beverly Hills, apologized profusely to Flash and me because, due to the very late hour, they had run out of the steak and lobster we wanted.

"Damian," I said, "you're breaking my heart."

We'd sat at Anami's bar for close to two hours. Sheri had called to say that she and the gang were making very little progress in rehearsals and we should order without her. She would join us when she could, or maybe, if rehearsals went on past midnight, she'd just go straight back to our hotel.

"This really sucks," she said.

"Tell me about it," I replied, unsure if she meant her missed dinner or *Lally's Place*.

Anami's, the most fashionable and exclusive restaurant in Beverly Hills for the moment, looked very much like a dozen or more other restaurants I had dined in: silk wallpaper, subdued lighting, fine dinnerware, too many plants.

Flash and I wore dark suits and sober ties to Anami's, so that people would think we were high-tech hotshots from San Francisco or Boeing sales reps from Seattle. Just so long as nobody thought we were in show business. Those people didn't wear ties and thought that the more mismatched their outfits looked, the more chic they were.

Producers and directors wore sports coats and open-necked shirts, with khakis and casual shoes, unless they had just come from a day of filming, when they would wear outdoors gear and a baseball cap.

Screenwriters wore windbreakers or Army surplus jackets. They certainly did not wear tweed jackets with suede patches on the elbows; that would be too corny even for them.

Actors wore sports apparel and didn't shave that often. They wanted to look masculine, fit and employed.

Actress wanted to look as though they were trying to go incognito so that their fans wouldn't recognize them. They wore hats and sunglasses and succeeded at looking anonymous. Easy enough to do; actresses, as often as not, don't look so glamorous without their makeup and hair specialists.

"This place is pretty new," Flash said. "It's competing well against Spago."

I surveyed the room. "It won't last."

"Are you kidding? It's packed to the titties."

"I'll bet they paid some *Michelin Guide* critic to come in here and give it four stars," I said. "That's why it's busy—people want to see what all the buzz is for."

"So what's the problem?"

"These fancy places that charge high prices? They're really going out of style. San Francisco had a dozen or so places like this one, and they're all gone because the business climate is all wrong. The people with money want casual dining and more modest prices. It's the same in Bayporte, and Bayporte is nobody's idea of a world-class restaurant city."

Damian came back and I said, "You don't have

what we want, so we'll just have a few more Canadian Comforts over ice. Bring us some coffee, too. It goes well with the liquor."

We sat and drank and eavesdropped on the conversations around us. Flash turned on his cell phone to record what we overheard when an agent said to someone:

"Richard still has some sex appeal left. Why can't we put him in something with Diane again? Of course, make them keep their clothes on. They're too old to be naked now."

We chuckled as we watched the producer hurry in and say to his fledgling actress, "Didn't mean to keep you waiting, sweetie. My daughter overdosed and my wife freaked out. They've both been stabilized. Aren't you *ravishing* tonight!"

Two wheeler-dealers strode past us, one of them saying, "There's no risk. There's never been any risk. I don't believe in risks. Let someone else take risks."

Two young women followed them, one saying to the other, "They gave his parking spot to someone else and said they would have security escort him out the door if he didn't get his boxes packed fast enough."

We finished drinking and left the restaurant. On the way back to the hotel, we pigged out at an All-American Burger drive-through. After saying goodnight to Flash, I returned to my suite and found Sheri on the sofa, morose.

"Hey, sweetie," she said as I gave her a little kiss. "This showbiz shit is wearing me out."

"Whatcha got there?" I asked, pointing to the document on her lap.

"It's what the bosses think of our show," she said

as I settled onto the sofa across from her.

"I know they've been hiring and firing actors and writers, then re-hiring some of them. Fighting like hell over everything."

Sheri nodded. "Right. Well, the latest thing is that some idiot from development checked us out and said, 'Where are the jokes?' We *had* jokes, you know, but everyone insists on changes. The writers churn out revisions till dawn, then some network executive from upstairs says, 'The show lacks charm.'

"So, they try to improve things by making Lally, my character, more empathic and sensitive. Change her from a hotel manager to a beauty shop owner or a pet shop proprietor. Then they changed her back to a hotel manager. Also, people are saying she shouldn't have HIV because there's nothing funny about AIDS."

"There's nothing funny about illness, period," I said. "Of course there's nothing funny about war, either, but M*A*S*H was a big hit."

"Oh, they think *Lally's Place* has much 'potential' and could become a 'blockbuster,' but we need to change things around quite a bit.

"The bosses insist that we deepen Lally and Addison as characters so that their friendship has credibility and substance, the bond that all great TV friendships have. They think it's not altogether necessary to have the two principals as friends when the story begins. It might be better if they were adversaries in some way and their friendship develops because they see value in having an ally to turn to and lean on in their cold, cruel world.

"The way we have it now, Lally is smart and sassy while Addison is simple but sweet, and the humor can come from each character's attempts at remaking the other."

I sat there and nodded. Sheri wasn't done with her rundown.

She tapped on the document in her lap. "They want us to emphasize the principals' personal histories. How and why did Lally and Addison come to be in this funky old hotel at this stage in their lives? Exploring this question will, for the show's viewers, address the matter of *why* life is so full of hassles and bullshit for Lally, Addison and everyone else in the world."

"Good luck with that," I muttered.

"'We need to convey the message of every successful buddy relationship: Separately we fail, but together we succeed.'"

"Well," I said, "I guess it was nice of them to tell you all that. They're trying to help you."

"Oh, there's plenty more in this document they gave me. I'm just giving you a summary. There's some serious nitpicking later on in these pages." She got up, sighed, and came over to me, offering her hand. "Let's go to bed. I hope I don't have nightmares about *Lally's Place*."

"I wish I could can them all," Sheri said over breakfast in our room. "The writers, directors and executive producers first." She slurped some coffee and swallowed a mouthful of scrambled eggs. "You know what? At first, I thought our director was fairly astute. He said, 'Always remember that the network is wrong. All successful shows happen *despite* the network executives who think they know everything.'" Sheri paused. "Of course, our director always does as the network says, so what does *he* know?"

"Maybe the show will be a smash despite him," I said.

"Do you know how many writers we've fired? Sixteen. They usually don't last more than a few days, and most of them don't understand much about humor. Here's an example: Say, 'I'm beat.'"

"I'm beat."

Sheri scowled. "*You're* beat? What about Iraq?"

She slapped the breakfast table and said, "That's a joke, son! Get it?"

I frowned. "That's one of the lines on the show?"

"That's one of *my* lines on the show." Then, "Earlier this week, a new group of hacks came in to 'improve' the script. They changed the line to, '*You're* beat? What about *this chick*?' And I was supposed to point at myself when I said '*this chick*.'"

"That's pretty dumb," I said.

"Dumb? It's fucking idiotic. I said to Sully Jackman, the director, 'No way in hell will I say *this chick*.' So Sully's like, 'Say it. It will be funny.' I said, 'Sully, if I say it, they'll laugh *at* me, not *with* me.' And he's like, 'So what? As long as they *laugh*.'"

"I hope you won that battle."

She nodded. "I did, and good for me. The line was stupid and at least *I* had the balls to say so."

"First Sean Penn, and now Sheri Rawson. You actors are temperamental little buggers, hey?"

She laughed. "But I'm just standing up for myself. Do you remember that comic Roseanne? She had her own sitcom, staffed by Canadian writers who didn't know how Americans talked. Roseanne had people fired over bad scripts, so she becomes the Bitch of Hollywood. I'm not her. I'm not throwing my weight around, telling everyone, 'It's my way or the highway.' I just don't want to go on national TV and say and do idiotic things."

I poured us both some more coffee and asked, "Who's the biggest pain in your ass over there?"

"The executive producers, Arnold Shapiro and Faith Podborsky. They need to be skinned alive, then beheaded. Those two insist on rewriting scripts, and I think they're both illiterate. Arnold dresses sort of like a cowboy who wants to look ridiculous, and Faith dresses all in black."

"Are the executive producers really allowed to rewrite the scripts?

"Yes. When I asked Faith about it, she said, 'We can rewrite the stuff because we know what works. After all, we used to write for *Thirtysomething*.'"

"Tough to argue with *those* kinds of creds," I said.

Sheri got up and started getting ready for the day.

"Come with me," she said. "Watch me rehearse. Meet the lovely people I've just told you about."

I declined. "I think I'll just hang out here and watch TV, diddle around on the Internet and order up room service."

Sheri shrugged. "Stay here if you want, but it'll be calm on the set. We all said some shit and I think we've cooled off."

She then told me about doing a *Lally* scene in which she had to walk across her living room to answer the phone. Arnold Shapiro stepped onto the set and insisted that they put a package of cigarettes on the table, and that Sheri take one out and light it before answering the phone.

"Absolutely not," Sheri told Arnold. "Meryl Streep might light up before answering the phone, and maybe Nicole Kidman or Julia Roberts or Angelina Jolie, but not me and not Lally."

"Please do it," Arnold said, nearly whimpering. "It would be *so* Lally to smoke while chatting on the phone."

"*Sully!*" Sheri hollered to Sully Jackman, the pilot's director. "Come settle this, please."

"Can't do it, babe," Sully said through his microphone in the control room. "I'm busy."

"Wimp," she muttered. To Arnold, she said, "I am *not* going to smoke in this show. Understand?"

"We can use herbal cigarettes," he said. "No nicotine, no danger of addiction."

"Herbal cigarettes smell like cow feces," Sheri said.

Faith got into the dispute. "Sheri, *we* know that smoking while on the phone would be right for Lally, even if *you* don't think so."

"Well, it's *my* lungs that's gonna get polluted and diseased, not yours. So why don't *you* just take a seat and shut the fuck up?" Sheri cackled as Faith went red-faced.

I knew that, in the TV industry, executive producers had plenty of discretion, especially over script matters, when the suits from the network were absent. The executive producers were an essential part of the team as they developed the pilot and tried to get it on the air. *Somebody* had to be in charge of the show from the beginning and stay with it during its run as a series, if it got that far.

The actors had no such hassles. They simply did

read-throughs, then the taping session. They would spend the rest of the week sleeping in, going for walks, shopping around for more prestigious agents and bitching about how Susan Sarandon got the movie part *they* wanted.

The director had it easy. He could spend most of his time golfing and playing tennis, then pop in, tape the show, and have a flunky email him a copy of the completed show.

Writers, of course, would just hammer out the same garbage that paid their bills, revise other writers' trash and check in the Guild to see what was going on. The writers would also rewrite segments of their own overlong, unwieldy novels they'd been working on for the past two decades.

"Arnold and Faith," Sheri told me, "will stay with *Lally's Place* as its overall bosses if the network gives it a go and orders thirteen. It'll be their baby and, if it becomes a hit, they may even be able to get a decent table at one of the better Beverly Hills restaurants."

"That's mighty keen," I said.

Sheri shuddered. "Can you imagine what kind of person it takes to supervise a sitcom? Executive producers don't have the imagination to create anything, so they just grab someone else's work and run with it. *Lally's Place* was thought up by some wretch out there who's probably pissed off as all hell because he told Arnold and Faith about it, and now they've basically stolen his idea. Not long ago Arnold and Faith were hack writers, no better than anyone else…and today they're executive producers." She shook her head and snarled. "I swear to you, Red, those two think that *Lally's Place* is Beowulf!"

"So," I asked, "do you smoke the cigarette while

you talk on the phone?"

Sheri threw back her head and laughed. "Those people do bring out the crazy Canuck in me." Then, "Do you know that bitch Faith said? After I told them I wouldn't smoke on the show, she said, 'Sheri, we can't have this conflict every day. Smoking the cigarette while talking on the phone may seem a minor issue to *you*, but to *us* it's called "character development." What is your background, anyway? It's certainly not acting, because you're not acting like a professional actor.'"

"Ouch," I said.

"Wait, there's more." Sheri made a pinched face and spoke in a goofy voice that I assumed were intended to mock Faith. "'You're a model from Canada, right, Sheri? Your husband is, or was, a football star, and your father is a rich industrialist. You have zero screen-acting experience. That explains why you're not getting with the fucking program here.

"'Remember, Sheri, that *you* are not the boss of this show, even though it may appear otherwise. Well, you don't run this show. Arnold and I *do*. Do we understand each other?'"

Sheri had stuck her middle finger in Faith's face and said, "Do you understand *this*?"

EIGHT

Over the following week, I seldom saw Sheri but did get updates on that tragedy-in-the-making called *Lally's Place*. I mostly confined myself to our hotel room—Sheri had suggested I take walks through Westwood or ride the buses just to explore Los Angeles' vastness. But I had already seen the Hollywood sign and Sunset Boulevard's billboards enough times. Besides, as a lazy bastard by nature, I enjoyed lying in bed with the remote control, flipping through 150 channels for hours at a time.

When I hit a rerun of *Happy Days* or *Three's Company*, I would think of Sheri, two dozen blocks away on the *Lally* set, trying to turn piss into lemonade. I believed in my wife and that her viewers would fall in love with her cover-girl face, bouncing breasts, heart-shaped bum and exuberant personality.

I felt like telling Arnold Shapiro and Faith Podborsky to rename their program *Sheri's Place*. Sheri wouldn't be playing Lally; my wife would be playing one facet of herself—and nobody did Sheri better than Sheri.

Occasionally, I turned off the TV and thought about other things that deserved some of my attention.

I had made a commitment to cover NFL games with Con Horwitz starting in mid-October, a week away, and I started feeling anxious about that.

I had agreed to a second career as a TV color man simply because it seemed a better option than selling cars or pimping myself out to public relations firms, as many other ex-athletes had done. I wanted to keep working if only to stay out of trouble. However, like my wife, I wanted to make sure I wanted to maintain my dignity in whatever I did. I dreaded being in the broadcast booth, letting Con Horwitz make a fool of me. After all, he had made a career out of making himself look dumb.

I felt better after ESPN honcho Mark Richardson flew in. He called from the Beverly Hills Hotel.

"I'm in town for a few days to help a couple of local affiliates get their shit together," he told me. "I want to see you for a drink, Red. When it's convenient for you."

It turned out that Mark had many other drink obligations, so we decided on a late afternoon that was convenient for *him*.

We had our drink in Westwood House's fancy lounge. Mark sat facing the lobby so that he could look past me in case Bono, Ringo Starr, George Clooney or Tiger Woods happened to appear.

"Have you eaten at the Chateau Marmont?" he asked, sipping his unsweetened iced tea. "Don't bother—it's overrated. I had a disappointing lunch at Dan Tana's, too. Plus, they sent me a white stretch limo, even though I wanted a smaller black one."

"Hard luck," I said.

Presently he finished his drink, took out his iPad and tapped on it a few times to finalize a few deals. "Did I tell you that I fired Abe this morning?"

"The guy who does color for Con Horwitz?"

"Yes. He made some objectionable remarks on the air, and we can't have that."

"Did he use profanity?" I asked, confused.

"No, nothing that bad. He just was too partisan, making his disappointment clear when the Giants played poorly."

I sighed, wondering how I would sound when covering an Invaders game and how Mark would feel if I got carried away.

"Did Abe really deserve to get fired?"

"Yes. He had a big mouth and a mediocre NFL career." Mark glanced at his platinum Rolex watch that must have cost more than most people earn in a year.

"Do you remember," he was saying now, "a guy up in Canada named Fergie Olver? He covered the Toronto Blue Jays until they canned him because he was such a Blue Jays fan. If Olver was going to last up there in the booth, he needed to cover the game and keep his personal feelings to himself, because he was just some mediocre Canadian broadcaster and nobody cared how he felt about the Blue Jays."

"I'll try to remember that," I said.

"Oh, not *you*, Red. You're different." Mark chuckled. "You're Red Crossley of the Invaders. You've earned the right to speak your mind, on or off the air."

"Can I say that a player got lazy or sloppy?"

"You can say whatever you want. Just no profanity."

I nodded. "I can leave the profanity at home."

"Your first game," he told me, "will be in Detroit when the Lions take on the Giants. That way, you'll be able to interview Painless O'Neal, who of course is indirectly responsible for your career change. We'll run the interview during a lull in the game and it will show everyone that you two are still friends."

"He came to visit me after he put me in the hospital. He said he was sorry," I told Mark

Richardson.

He smiled. "Painless is a class act. So, are we excited about this or what?"

"We're excited," I said.

"Welcome to the world of TV!" He reached over and shook my hand.

Soon after Richard left, Flash came into the lounge and sat with me. He, too, had scarcely ventured out of his room upstairs. He needed to finish his NFL piece for *Playboy* so they could publish it in their December or January issue.

"Their idea," he said, "is to run my piece during the postseason, so people will get to read about what bullshit the NFL is just when they're most interested in it."

I ran down my meeting with Mark Richardson.

"Good deal," Flash said. "Do you know why he fired Abe Charles?"

"Because he sucked?"

"No, man, he didn't suck. The problem was that Charles had been hired by someone else, and Richardson, the new boss, needed to clean house a bit by getting rid of the previous honcho's hires and replacing them with his own hires.." Flash smiled. "As long as *he's* in, *you're* in."

L.T. Briggs called Flash in his hotel room while I was there. "Put Red on the extension. I have great news, and I want to share it with both of you."

I got on the extension. "I'm here, Coach. Tell me something good."

"Gennelmen," he said, "Northup is going to win the Canadian title next year. Not just the regional, but the national. The Kodiaks will reign supreme."

Flash said, "Coach, are you drunk?"

"I'm pissed out of my tree," he said, swallowing a tiny laugh. "But I have reason to be celebrating my good news with a couple of old friends and eternal Kodiaks."

"So tell us," I said.

"Oh, yeah. I'm going to have Scoliosis Robinson *and* DeShonn Jones on my team."

"For real?" I asked.

"No shit here, Red." He farted loudly, put his hand over the phone's speaker and said to his wife, "Damn, honey, did you hear *that* one?"

"Details, Coach," Flash said. "How did you get them?"

"Getting Scoliosis was easy enough. Lord Larry Rawson took out his checkbook and said, 'L.T., you go get that spade no matter how much it costs.' I bought Scoliosis a Tesla Roadster and gave him credit cards every color of the rainbow. Once he gets here, he's going to have more white vag than he's ever dreamed of."

L.T. said that DeShonn Jones, the lightning-fast wide receiver many colleges wanted, had signed with Seattle's University of Washington—U. Dub—but dropped out altogether. DeShonn told the media that he had been miserable and depressed in cold, rainy Seattle, which was another way of saying that they expected him to attend classes and write term papers. Also, he had learned that his meal allowance of $5,000 per month was half the amount the University of Oregon paid its star wide receiver.

So DeShonn had withdrawn from school and driven back to Arkansas in the white Mercedes U. Dub had given him. He moved back in with his family and bided his time watching the big-screen TV a Washington alumnus had paid for.

"Washington's coaches were pissed that DeShonn fucked them over like that," L.T. said on the phone, chuckling. "That car was damned expensive. But they couldn't bitch about it, because then they would have to admit they broke the rules by bribing him with a car."

"Just like how you gave Scoliosis that Roadster," Flash said.

"Well," L.T. said, "let's just hope nobody asks too many questions about we got both those boys to attend Northup."

He told us that DeShonn, disappointed over getting a very good deal instead of a great one from U. Dub., had complained of myriad minor health problems—a sore this, an aching that—and sat on the sidelines as he covertly pursued opportunities at other schools.

"DeShonn didn't play *one single down* for the Washington Huskies," L.T. noted. "So he can sit out this season and sign with us next season."

"Why are you so absolutely sure that things will work out for you?" I asked.

"Because Lord Larry Rawson says so. I think he's gotten to the point where he's done everything with his mining-and-minerals business, so now he's looking at Northup and thinking, 'We've got to make those Kodiaks the best in Canada before I croak.' Maybe he thinks if we can turn our team into some kind of powerhouse, the school will rename its stadium Rawson Field."

L.T. explained that Lord Larry's big plan for the Kodiaks included making Rickey Robinson, Scoliosis' older brother, an "executive assistant" at Rawson Enterprises. Rickey had a big office next to Lord Larry's and received a higher salary than a dozen Rawson receptionists and secretaries combined.

"What does Rickey know about mining?" Flash asked.

"Rickey knows Scoliosis," said L.T., "and Scoliosis knows football."

"Oh," Flash and I said in unison.

"Rickey's job is to get Scoliosis and DeShonn into my backfield. Just this morning, Rickey called me from wherever the fuck DeShonn lives. He says our negotiations are in good shape so far. It's all about money now, and you *know* Lord Larry can deal with *that*."

"Lord Larry rules," Flash said. "You can't stop him when he's found something he wants to buy."

"Damn straight and thank goodness," said L.T. Then, "Can you guess how it's gonna be for me to have Scoliosis Robinson and DeShonn Jones in my backfield? I'm gonna have a hard-on all day and half the night!"

"So Rickey just hangs out in his office most of the day," I asked, "when he's not down south negotiating with DeShonn?"

"Lord Larry says Rickey is a geo-something by profession and has a framed diploma on his wall. Might be bullshit, but who cares?"

Flash said, "You have a great idea here and you may make the Kodiaks the greatest thing in Canadian sports history if you don't get caught breaking the rules and go to jail."

L.T. laughed. "Nobody goes to jail for trying to build a better college football team."

I admitted to L.T. that one thing kept nagging at me while making me smile with the deepest gratification. I had trouble picturing a black man such as Rickey Robinson ensconced in an office at lily-white Rawson Enterprises, not far from Placid Oaks Country Club, right in the middle of downtown Bayporte, Great Elizabeth, Canada.

"I know this isn't Mississippi in 'Sixty-two, but still…"

"No worries here, Red," L.T. said. "Everybody understands why Rickey's up there, making big bucks while sitting on his ass most of the time. Lord Larry wants a winning Kodiaks team, and Rickey can deliver it."

Sheri was on the rag the next morning, but I empathized with her. The big *Lally* taping would happen that evening at seven o'clock, and her day would be full long before the director yelled, "Action!" Her hair, for one thing, had to be washed and set; and what about wardrobe? How would Lally be dressed—in jeans and a T-shirt, or in fancy, funky stuff she'd bought at a secondhand store? They had scheduled two dress rehearsals for that day…and who had the bright idea of turning the taping into a major media event?

Normally, pilots were performed before studio audiences comprising people literally off the street, tourists and other passersby pulled in by studio flunkies, aggressive as carnival hucksters, who barked, "Come right in and watch TV history being made!"

Not *Lally's Place*. In its audience, Flash and I would sit with at least a dozen network know-nothings who kept residences in Los Angeles and Manhattan. Lord Larry and Lady Joy would fly in on their private jet. Jack and Kathleen Piros were coming in on *their* jet. Probably, too, some real actors would sit in, to see what the *Lally's Place* buzz was about.

Sheri tried not to obsess over it. But now she started fretting over her refusal to say *this chick* and how to make Arnold Shapiro and Faith Podborsky understand that she, Sheri Rawson, had as much creative control over the show as they did.

In our hotel room, she changed jeans, T-shirts and brassieres three times. "I would stop this *Lally* shit and just go back home if it weren't for Sully."

"Who's Sully?" I asked as I tapped away on my iPad.

"Sully Jackman, Bubba. My director. I've told you about him. How's your concussion?"

Bubba, our private joke, was her nickname for me whenever I did or said something irretrievably stupid, which happened entirely too often. She had read about obese, dim-witted American Southerners' being called Bubba, and decided to apply it to me, a dim-witted western Canadian.

"I thought you said Sully sucked," I said to my wife as she fastened her favorite brassiere and admired her pushed-up breasts in the mirror.

"I did, but I've changed my mind. He's smart and diplomatic. He understands TV comedy. I like him a lot."

"Why was he being such a prick at first?"

She shrugged. "He was being enigmatic. I guess hbecomes whoever he needs to be depending on the situation."

"Is he handsome?"

"I guess. I mean, they all look like Rhett Butler in this town, hey? Even the directors."

"I suppose his harelip and leprosy don't matter to you," I said.

"He's better-looking than you, he has a better mind and degrees from all the best colleges, and he's the fuck of the century." She fastened her jeans, pulled on her T-shirt, whirled around to give me a kiss and went away.

NINE

In our hotel room, Lord Larry Rawson poured himself another splash of Canadian Comfort over ice and said, "I know for an absolute fact that Mary Tyler Moore is dead."

"Wrong," said Flash. "She's nearly blind from diabetes but still alive. Her best friend on the show, Rhoda, is dead."

"Mary's dead, too," Lord Larry repeated.

A bunch of us were having an informal little party in our hotel suite: Lord Larry. Lady Joy, Jack and Kathleen Piros, plus Flash and me. I had ordered up a couple of bottles of Canadian Comfort so that we might self-medicate for that evening's taping of *Lally*.

I knew I could not go into that studio and watch my wife perform in front of several hundred people unless I was good and pissed. Flash, Jack and Lord Larry had the same idea.

Lord Larry, Jack, Flash and I stood in the middle of our suite's living room. in one corner, Kathleen Piros and Lady Joy lay on sofas, bitching about the cost of Louis Vuitton accessories.

"Hey, Gortton," Lord Larry was saying now, "you're the world's greatest expert on practically everything, so tell me why Mary Tyler Moore is still alive."

Flash shrugged. "Same reason you and I are still here. Not our time yet."

"How do you know she's still alive? Did you go down on her last night or something?"

Flash threw back his head and laughed.

"You didn't eat her pussy last night," Lord Larry

said, "because she's dead. She croaked about the same time as Bob Hope, that funny guy who kept working long after he stopped being funny. I got sick of Bob Hope. I can't remember laughing at any of his jokes." He paused. "I lost interest in show business after Clint Eastwood died."

"Has Clint Eastwood died?" I looked from Lord Larry to Flash.

Lord Larry glowered at me.

I shook my head. "How did Eastwood die? When?"

"Don't know how or when," said Lord Larry, "but I know he did, just like Mary Tyler Moore."

I said to Jack Piros, "She's not dead, is she?"

"If Lord Larry says so, he must've heard it somewhere."

Lord Larry said, "Flash, tell me something: If she isn't dead, why isn't she on TV any more?"

"Maybe she's retired," he replied. "Retired isn't the same as dead."

Lady Joy and Kathleen Piros got off their sofas and joined the rest of us.

"Has someone been talking about Mary Tyler Moore?" Lady Joy asked.

"We're trying to figure out if she's still alive," I said.

"What difference does it make?" Lady Joy asked.

Flash went over and lay down on the sofa Lady Joy had just vacated. He stretched out and chuckled. "Lady Joy has a point. Who cares if Mary Tyler Moore is dead? Mary Tyler Moore cares. Do *you* give a shit, Red?"

"*I'm* starting to give a shit," Jack Piros said. "You got a computer here? We can go online and check it out."

"You know who I liked even more than Clint Eastwood?" said Lord Larry. "John Wayne! I could watch his movies all day and half the night."

"That's because he just kept on making the same movie for years," said Flash.

"The same movie? How do you figure that?" I asked, reaching for the Canadian Comfort.

"I know people out here who know about screenplays. On page thirty-five, the Duke stands up in his Western gear and tells the audience what the movie is all about. On page ninety-five, he does pretty much the same thing all over again. By page one-hundred-thirty, the movie ends and the Duke wanders off into the sunset."

Lord Larry nodded. "That was quite a good movie, too. Clint Eastwood may not have been in it, but it was still bloody good."

"They don't make those kinds of movies anymore," said Jack Piros, sighing. "They don't make them that way because they can't. The movie stars today are no taller than five-eight, so they no longer appear larger than life."

"Sheri keeps bitching about the 'trade magazines,'" Lord Larry said. "What are they?"

"They're called *Variety* and *The Hollywood Reporter*," said Jack Piros.

Lord Larry nodded. "Yeah. Those trade magazines should run a list of who's dead and who's alive, so we can keep track of such things."

Flash said, "Damn right, Larry. If Mary Tyler Moore is still alive, the world needs to know about it."

"It would help," Lord Larry said, "if the trades

printed a last-page list of who's still around. Nothing fancy, but if they *knew* that these celebrities were still alive, make sure they're on the list."

Flash raised his glass to toast Lord Larry. "That's the ticket, Larry. Maybe I'll email the trades tomorrow and urge them to start publishing that list."

...

We took limousines to the studio to watch Sheri act. We went in and kept quiet because the red lights were on and taping was in progress. Sheri, as Lally, got a decent-sized laugh by saying, "*You're* beat? What about Iraq?" Now she stepped away from Addison, played by Sasha Rothman, to greet a couple who had just entered the lobby and wanted to know about rates and availability at Lally's Place.

We sat on the small hard seats and folded our coats over our laps as a voice sounded over the public-address system.

"That line is better than what we have," the voice said. "We'll end the scene with that. Let's set up for the dining room."

We were in the second row. Every audience seat in the studio held an ass, and each ass seemed to belong to someone who wanted to laugh at *Lally's Place* whether it was funny or not, judging by the slightly strained guffaws at the Iraq joke. The set had three parts, side by side: The lobby of the hotel; the hotel's coffee shop; and Lally's apartment (the hotel's proprietor did not reside on the premises).

To our left sat the network executives who, as part of their jobs, flew every other week from Los Angeles to New York City, or vice versa. Now they sat near us, their hands folded in their laps, lips pursed as their flunkies sat next to them, scribbling away on yellow legal pads. I had seen happier people at funerals.

Down in front of us sat two characters we recognized immediately: Arnold Shapiro and Faith Podborsky, the executive producers of *Lally's Place*.

Arnold Shapiro, a tall, skinny man pushing fifty, wore a fringed leather jacket, jeans and a Stetson hat, even though he, like John Wayne, had never been anywhere near a ranch.

Faith Podborsky reminded me of Mike Myers' *Saturday Night Live* character Dieter from the sketch *Sprockets*. With her shiny black hair, black clothes and glasses, she could have passed for Dieter's kid sister. She drew on a skinny cigar despite the NO SMOKING sign on the wall.

I leaned over a bit to Lord Larry, who sat beside me, and muttered, "The odd couple down there? They're not laughing. That's bad news."

"They both look constipated," he retorted. "Does that woman always dress in black? Who does she think she is, Andy Warhol?" Then, "Why is she smoking? Does she think that 'No Smoking' applies to everyone but her?"

The taping resumed. An overhead electric sign said ON THE AIR in large, lurid red letters. A man wearing headphones flashed a few hand signals at Sheri, who stood alongside Addison. Sheri/Lally wore a splendid Armani or Versace outfit; I wondered how a fleabag hotel operator could afford such chic apparel. The audience probably would, too, if *Lally's Place* ever became a series.

Sheri strode across her living room, stopped at her coffee table and picked up a small, square object. She spun around and faced Sasha/Addison. "Brad Pitt has been here!"

Only Flash and I laughed. Sasha, staying in character, nearly laughed.

"Is that a pack of cigarettes?" Sasha/Addison said, swallowing a chuckle.

"Yes it is!" said Sheri. "Only three men would leave a half-empty pack of Newports on someone's coffee table: Tom Cruise, Brad Pitt and Mark Wahlberg."

"Maybe," said Sasha, "it was Cruise or Wahlberg."

"No. Those guys are too short to reach my coffee table."

I looked over at Arnold and Faith, who simply stared at the actors, as if this performance were in a foreign language.

Sheri and Sasha started improvising.

"Mark Wahlberg," said Sasha, "has grown into a fine actor. Didn't you see him in *Pain and Gain*?"

"Nope," said Sheri.

"Why the hell not?"

"Because," Sheri retorted, "I already know how to work out."

I leaned over and whispered to Flash, "Pretty bad, eh?"

"Even worse," he replied.

On the set, Sasha lit a clove cigarette and said, "Lally, I've been thinking that we should stop having the exterminator come in to spray the hotel."

"Why? Is it too expensive?"

"Yes, and I'm starting to think that the bugs have become immune to the insecticide. They like it. It's like candy to them."

"By the way, Eddie called you and left a message," said Sasha.

Lally frowned. "My ex called me. Why?"

"He's still your husband till your divorce becomes final. He mentioned that on the phone."

"Eddie," Lally said, "is a douche bag."

I wasn't sure if the folks upstairs in Standards and Practices would let "douche bag" slip by.

"Eddie thinks you're being difficult about the divorce just because he's now dating a much younger woman," Sasha said.

"'A much younger woman'? She's a fetus in candy pants."

I doubted that line, too, would get past the censors.

Arnold Shapiro and Faith Podborsky stood up, with loud sighs and shaking heads, and traipsed up the aisle.

In the final scene, the producers had ordered a script change: the transgendered prostitute became a male hipster in skinny jeans and an oversized scarf. The guy had entered the coffee shop to have dinner, the idea being that the hipster would be someone the under-forty viewers could relate to.

Sheri caught my eye and rolled hers. I knew she wouldn't like the hipster. I wondered how she would deal with him.

She looked him up and down. "Are you here to eat, or do you just want to sit down and sneer at everyone?"

The hipster sat at a table and perused the menu. "Do you have anything totally vegan? I don't believe in eating the flesh of dead animals."

"Yeah, we got vegan. We got vegetarian, too, and fruitarian." Sheri grabbed a plate from a passing server and set in in front of the hipster. "How's that?"

"Wow. Cool." The hipster looked up at her.

"What's in it?"

"I'm not sure. But I think it's edible."

Big laugh from the audience. Even the crew doubled over.

"That's it," said the director over the P.A. system. "That's a wrap."

The audience cheered, whistled and applauded. The hipster stood up and bowed, thinking their praise was for him.

Flash and I felt relieved for Sheri. We resolved never again to have anything to do with a situation comedy unless someone we loved, or at least knew well, had a big part in it.

Lord Larry said, "I liked that. Sheri sure made a fool of that fairy."

Lady Joy said to Kathleen Piros, "That casual outfit she had on? I swear it was by John Galliano. At first I thought it might have been by Versace or Chanel, but now I'm sure it was Galliano. We met him at a party in Coral Gables. Such a lovely man!"

"He's so imaginative and colorful in his designs," Kathleen said. "Sometimes the Italians get inhibited and boring."

Jack Piros said, "I didn't know Sasha was still acting. I thought she had married some rich guy and retired, like she should have."

The Rawsons and Piroses decided to go to Spago. "Just for the hell of it," said Jack. "So I can say I've been there. Plus, there's no way in hell they'll turn us away, especially if Larry is in our party."

Flash and I waited for Sheri. We also wanted to meet the show's director, Sully Jackman, a handsome man in his thirties. He had an effeminate way of swiveling his hips when he walked, and he spoke with a funny accent. But he must have been straight, judging by the way Sheri threw her arms around him when he appeared.

Flash and I stood on the stage, muttering to each other about how hot and uncomfortable actors must be, standing under those hot lights and delivering those dumb lines.

The place now seemed deserted as Sheri emerged in her own clothes and threw herself into my arms. I gathered her up and was about to plant a nice big juicy one on her when Sully, who'd just locked up the control room, said, "Lallybaby!"

My wife pried herself away from me and hopped into Sully's arms. They exchanged a long, lip-smacking kiss.

Another husband might have objected to their kiss and punched the man in the nose. But I understood that in Hollywood, people kissed each other's lips. And asses.

"She did a good job, eh?" I said while Sully kept busy kissing my wife.

"A comedic star is born," said Flash.

"She's beyond the highest praise," Sully said once he got his lips off my missus.

Presently Arnold Shapiro and Faith Podborsky returned with their flunkies and a few network heavies. Why? Did they want to beat the shit out of Sheri or Sully, or both?

A network heavy introduced himself to Flash and me. He told us he was old enough to remember when Los Angeles had two football franchises, and now it had none. As both an Angeleno and New Yorker, he now rooted for the New York Giants.

"Do you think the Giants will win another Super

Bowl anytime soon?" he asked Flash.

"I hope not," said Flash.

Most of us sauntered into the living room of the *Lally* set and settled down. Arnold Shapiro and Faith Podborsky stood off to the side with their flunkies, as if afraid of the network heavies. Some of those heavies did seem intimidating, or at least supremely self-important, but my guess was that the really powerful people had stayed back in Manhattan

Nobody said anything to the group until Sully Jackman exclaimed, "I think we have a hit!"

The heavies cleared their throats.

"It has potential," said one.

"The potential is there," agreed a woman in a smart dark suit.

"So we'll go so far as to use the word 'potential'?" asked one of the heavies.

The first heavy nodded. "That seems fair. The pilot has much potential. It needs more jokes."

The dark-suited woman nodded. "More jokes and more Lally. She's very charming."

The first heavy said, "But I don't think we can give it a green light just yet."

The woman said, "Maybe a semi-green light."

The second heavy said, "We can give it a green light, a semi-green light or no green light at all. We have all of those options."

The first heavy said, "All of our options are open. We should go with a semi-green light."

The woman nodded. "Right. More jokes, more charm, more Lally."

The first heavy said to Sully Jackman, "Before I fly back to New York and tell them to green-light this project, you need to tell me if you'll be available to do thirteen."

"Maybe. I can definitely do seven or eight. I've been talking to Sony about a feature starring Scarlett Johansson, but nothing's settled yet, especially the budget. With movies, deals may fall apart at any time."

Sully went back to Westwood House with us for a nightcap at the bar.

"The network will want thirteen episodes," he said. "Those heavies back at the studio? They were full of bullshit, just a bunch of posers who had no real authority. The real bosses are back in New York and they're desperate for *Lally's Place*. I know this because an old friend of mine from USC Film School is one of those bosses and he's told me more than I had a right to know. The network wants the show as a mid-season replacement because it has very little confidence in the legs of its announced fall schedule.

"Even if *Lally* were the most odious piece of poo in TV history, which it isn't, its lack of quality would matter very, very little. The pilot really isn't that bad," Sully explained. "In fact, I would say it is somewhat better than many others I've had to sit through." He smiled at Sheri. "You have a great sense of comic timing. If *Lally* goes, it will be because its star has so much presence. You're already semi-famous as a model, so viewers will want to check you out to see if you can act as well as you do billboard and magazine cheesecake.

"Yes, sir, *Lally's Place* is as good as on the air."

CBS would certainly cancel two of its shows, *Weekend Homes* and *Paco*. *Lally's Place* would get one of those slots and *Celebrity Shopping Sprees* the other.

The network was juggling its whole schedule, Sully

told us.

Too School for Cool would move from Friday night to Thursday night. *Buff and Cut*, the hit comedy about two bodybuilders who succeed despite themselves as operators of a fashionable Miami Beach health club, would move to Saturday night.

CBS wanted to own Saturday night by running its best shows one after another. They would start off the fun with *Break Dancing Fools*, followed by *It's All Good* and *The Devil Next Door*, which had dominated the Neilsens for the past three seasons.

"Lally would entertain America right after *The Devil Next Door* and just before the late-night news," Sully said. He winked at Sheri. "Really, it's a whammo lineup. *Lally* will become a hit. You and I are going to have a regular gig for the next few years."

"I would be happier," Sheri said, "if they would put us on *before* a huge hit like *The Devil Next Door*. Before the late news? That just seems too *late* for prime time." She held up her empty glass, caught the barkeep's eye and nodded, smiling.

"So," Flash said to Sheri, "I need to get this straight. You are an actor now, right?"

She shrugged. "Looks like."

Flash turned to me. "Now she's an actor, Red. What is to be done about Sheri Rawson Crossley?"

"Damned if *I* know."

The three of us laughed hard, and Sheri gave each of us a kiss.

We made faces at each other and kept bursting out laughing, as if we'd just smoked some damn good shit and everything was a joke. We had done that all our lives—laughed our asses off at things that were hardly funny to those unlucky enough to be outside our little family of three.

"Don't mind us, Sully," she said. "We're just three hicks from Canada who think that life is one big bloody joke."

PART TWO

TEN

Mark Richardson sent me to Detroit to cover my first game with Con Horwitz. As NFL cities go, I've had very little use for Detroit. To me, a trip to Motor City consisted of a few nights in a hotel suite, a few hours of NFL action on a carpet and an icy flight *out of there.*

In my conversations about Detroit, I had always felt awkward, even speechless, around sports reporters who actually knew the city and had something good to say about it.

But just as soon as I lumbered from the aircraft into Detroit Metro Airport, I found a reason to believe that this trip—my first there as someone other than a jock—might have some unexpected perks.

Tia Gomez stood waiting for me.

My overnight bag hung from my shoulder when she walked up to me in the airport's vast lobby.

"Hi, Red," she said. "Welcome to my nightmare."

She told me her name and that she worked for ESPN as a stage manager.

"You see," she confided, "I'm not really supposed to be here at the airport, doing this...but come *on!* Red Crossley of the Invaders? Like I'm going to turn this down?"

All of this happened a year ago. As a drinker, sometimes I forget. Worse, I remember things that have never happened. But I think I remember that first meeting with Tia Gomez on that insufferably frigid Detroit morning. Or was it afternoon?

She was a friendly, affable young lady in her middle twenties who was also drop-dead beautiful.

As Tia drove me to my suite at Renaissance

Center, she told me things about herself and I listened as hard as I could, as I always did when beautiful women told me personal shit about themselves.

She had graduated from the University of Texas at Austin with a bachelor's degree in communications. She'd spent her childhood in Taos, New Mexico, but after graduating from Austin, she'd gotten a secretarial job at ESPN's Dallas affiliate because she wanted a TV career.

"A secretary with an Austin degree! How humbling!" she said with a laugh. They soon promoted her to production assistant or production associate. "It's also known as being a flunky, but at least they taught me about TV production, which was what I wanted."

"And now you're a 'stage manager,'" I said. "Is that better than being a flunky?"

"Hell yes. When we're live, I'm *alive*."

"So this ESPN NFL game is a big deal for you."

"The biggest."

Tia would spend the game inside the broadcast booth with Con Horwitz and me, giving us promo cards and cues and making sure Con and I didn't try to kill each other.

"I'll be keeping your coffee cup full for the rest of the season," she said. "Hope you can learn to cope with me."

I must admit that, during most of the drive from the airport to RenCen, I forgot I was married.

As we headed through gray, frosty, grimy downtown Detroit, I said, "This place really is dead on the weekends, eh?"

"It's always dead. So many of these skyscrapers are abandoned and boarded up. Not much here except poverty and despair." She paused. "You've already been here lots of times, right?"

"Yeah, but usually I'm just playing football or getting drunk. I haven't done any sightseeing."

"I got into town about a month ago, to get things ready for this broadcast."

As soon as we got to RenCen, Tia explained that my obligations that day were many and varied. As the TV color man, I had to see Ward Jimmins, the Lions' head coach, in his office; Cody Thomas, the Giants' head coach, wanted me to drop by *his* RenCen suite and wish him well. Fortunately, all the Giants were staying two minutes from my room, so I had easy access to Painless O'Neal for that interview ESPN wanted.

"I spoke to Painless," Tia said. "He's glad you're felling better and looks forward to your interview."

"He's an old friend."

"He's the guy who gave you that concussion, right?"

I nodded.

Tia told me that Con Horwitz would be flying in on someone's private jet. Con had a speaking engagement in another city and would be whisked from the lectern to the airport, fly out here, have dinner with me and a few others, spend the night in a deluxe RenCen suite, then head back to the airport to fly to another city, to deliver the same speech to a different audience. Or something like that.

"Have you two met?" she asked me.

"Haven't had the pleasure thus far."

"He'll bitch nonstop about everything, starting with his suite."

"Does he know who's playing?" I asked her. "Will

he know he's in Detroit?"

Tia laughed. "He does come across as being unprepared."

"He does a bit. Abrasive, too."

She repeated that I would be having dinner in RenCen's gourmet restaurant with Con Horwitz and a few other ESPN big shots supervising the game coverage.

"What about you?" I asked her.

Tia shrugged. Tall and slim, she had big, smoldering dark eyes, thick, silky black hair and a wide, gleaming smile.

"I'll fend for myself," she told me.

"Why?"

"Because," she said, "I'm just a stage manager. Producers and broadcasters get fancy dinners."

"Bullshit," I said. "You're eating with us tonight."

"Con and the bosses won't like that."

"Fuck 'em."

Insisting that Tia Gomez have dinner with us seemed, at that time, a perfectly innocuous, and even big-hearted, thing to do. To me, saying, "Sorry, Tia, you can't dine with us because you're not important enough," was tantamount to saying to a black friend, "Leroy, you can't drop your deuce here because this washroom is for whites only, so you'll have to use that swamp over there."

Regardless of what Flash Gortton would say much later on about my motives concerning Tia, I am pretty sure I would have insisted that my stage manager join us for dinner regardless of that person's gender, age, race or physical appearance.

"You invited her to dinner as a way of getting into her pants," Flash said in retrospect. "You were going to try to bang Tia silly and lie about it to Sheri."

Maybe he had it right.

Before TV dumbed down the world, people didn't call NFL coaches geniuses. Coaches received praise as clever, crafty and a dozen other adjectives. Coaches didn't toot their own horns because they didn't know how; they just shoved their players out there and told them to play football.

Now, every NFL coach is a genius. He speaks a foreign language; football code is as incomprehensible to most of us as what a team of doctors and nurses might say in an operating room—and has many people, visible and otherwise, who will do as he says. His computerized scouting system does more good than bad, his community supports him, his family doesn't hate him. He has earned his players' respect and seldom panics in front of them. Finally, his background is ambiguous and he seems to possess some sort of esoteric knowledge that he acquired from Bill Walsh or Don Shula.

But the main reason he's a genius is that TV and radio have said so.

Of course, many of these geniuses do things that confuse the rest of us. If these guys are, indeed, geniuses, why do they all use the same strategy? They establish their running games, then throw passes. They claim they win games on defense. They can't answer the simplest questions until they've looked at the video footage of plays they've already seen.

I mean, WTF?

When I played for the Invaders and we lost a game, I knew it was usually because one of our boys fell asleep and forgot to block a rusher or failed to hang onto a pass when it hit him in the numbers. When we won, our quarterback ignored our game plan and got the ball into the end zone.

If the San Francisco 49ers of the 1980s had rigidly adhered to Bill Walsh's game plan, they would have lost at least two of their four Super Bowls, and probably dropped more than four NFC Championship games. They would have kept running Roger Craig until he dropped dead from exhaustion. But Joe Montana, their quarterback, believed that his team needed, more than anything else. to score some touchdowns. So he took the snap, drifted back into the pocket and discovered that a huge lane had just split open right in front of him. He tucked the ball into the crook of his arm and scampered 25 yards into the opponents' end zone.

Then they called Bill Walsh a genius.

Eddie Lowelling had been a genius when Vernon Braithwaite, being chased by three gigantic lineman, had thrown the ball down the field and Flash Gortton managed to catch it.

I thought about these things as I sat in the office of Ward Jimmins, Detroit's new head coach. Jimmins, a tall, stocky Bill Gates lookalike, said, with some smugness, that he relied on computers to do much of his job. "It's all about data. Who's the other team? How big are their guys? We feed it all into the computer and it tells us the best way to play."

I wished him well and added that I hoped se didn't encounter too many opponents who did things the old-fashioned way, like emphasizing fundamentals.

He shrugged. "Fundamentals are overrated. Just let the computers take over. Say, how are you healing up? That Painless popped you a pretty hard one, huh?"

"Feeling OK now, Coach."

Jimmins shook his head. "Wouldn't have happened if the Invaders had gone high-tech like us."

I grinned a bit at the image of the bloodthirsty young lineman Ward Jimmins had been years earlier when he played for the Green Bay Packers. Now a middle-aged man who espoused the notion of letting a computer add up the sum of his team's parts and predict the winner of games that way, he probably would lose his job soon unless, by some miracle, his computer was right most of the time.

After that, I went back to the RenCen hotel and had a beer in my room. Then I got back into the elevator and went up two floors to say hidy to Cody Thomas, the Giants' head coach.

"Defense is the word, Red," he told me in his room, which was bigger and better than mine. "We blitz as a natural course of action, just to make sure that their quarterback doesn't feel safe out there. If one of their wide receivers is playing too well, we'll double-team him. Our thing is to keep them out of the end zone; if we do that, we'll usually score *something*, and that will usually be enough to win."

"The Eagles beat up on you pretty good last week," I reminded him, putting him on the spot and enjoying his shrug.

"Like I say, Red, we do our best to keep them out of the end zone, but sometimes they get in anyway. We all have days when things simply don't work for us."

"Zebras did you a few favors that day."

"Oh, they threw a few markers that gave us good field position. They take plenty of flak from everyone, but overall I would say they earn their keep."

"Are they ethical? Are they nonpartisan?"

Thomas smiled and shook his head. "*Our* referees? They're beyond reproach, Red. They make bad calls as often as good ones, but who among us is perfect?"

ELEVEN

People at Anami's were so drunk and happy that I could scarcely hear Sheri's voice when I called her.

"Good news, Red!" she shouted into her iPhone. "They've ordered thirteen episodes! *Lally's Place* will premiere in January!"

"Congrats!" I shouted back. "A star is born!"

"Not yet. We'll still have to get high ratings, and there's no guarantee that will happen."

Arnold Shapiro and Faith Podborsky were elsewhere, she said, having their own celebration. The *Lally* scripts needed to be much better, and that meant somehow decreasing the involvement of Arnold and Faith.

"Sheri," I asked her, "what happens now? What happens to you, me and us?"

She said she would definitely be staying at Westwood House for another several months, and longer if the show received the desired ratings. They would be eager to start shooting for next fall.

"I'll fly up to Bayporte on the weekends to see you if you're there," my wife told me. "You can fly down to see me at the hotel when I'm here. We'll have to make do with phone calls if you're there and I'm here."

That sounds perfectly shitty, I felt like telling her. But I didn't want to sound whiny while she and her *Lally* colleagues celebrated.

"Let's keep our fingers crossed that you get some better scripts," I said.

"Sully is going to revise some of them. Make them funnier."

"Who's Sully?"

"Sully Jackman, Bubba."

"Yeah. The fuck of the century."

Sheri swallowed a tiny, boozy giggle.

"I'm trying to stab Arnold and Faith in the back. Get them canned as executive producers and let Sully take over. He could do big things for this show."

"Is Sasha Rothman there? I'd like to congratulate her."

"She's busy. In the can or something. I'll tell her you said, 'Break a leg, girlfriend.' How are things in Detroit? Getting ready for your big day? Keeping warm?"

I told her I had met Con Horwitz as well as the director, producer and stage manager.

"Must have been awful, getting off the plane and not knowing anyone," Sheri said.

I said our stage manager met me at the airport.

"Stage manager? What's he like?"

I told her he was a tall Hispanic named Tino Gomez.

"Nice guy?" she asked.

You don't want to know.

"I'll bet Con is a prick," she said.

"I can put up with them if they can put up with me."

"Listen, sweetie, some people want to take pictures with me, so I'll hang up now. Behave yourself. Make sure you get a DVD of the game so Sully and I can check you out."

Click.

I tossed and turned most of that night. After

staring at the TV, then mentally and manually masturbating, I fell into a shallow sleep at close to four in the morning. I felt anxious about covering that game with Con Horwitz, naturally, and disliked my wife's affection for and admiration of Sully Jackman. I also hated her "I'll fly to you and you'll fly to me" shit if her *Lally* thing kept her in southern California indefinitely. But I had some guilt I needed to look in the eye and say hidy to.

I had lied to my wife about my stage manager's gender and name, and a little voice inside my head said, *That was a chickenshit thing to do, Red.* I hadn't laid a hand on Tia Gomez—yet. Why such remorse?

My remorse came from flirting with Tia, and why had I done that? Because she was a sexy young thing and I was a male—and all males who liked women had that little devil inside saying, *Fuck her! Fuck her brains out!*

As one of Uncle Rex's wives once said to her man, "You could no more get the cheating out of your dick than I could teach a bear not to shit in the woods." Well, yes. Men were cheaters and women were bitches. Hook up with one of them and take your chances.

. . .

"Wow! Unbelievable! Red Crossley, what do they say about those kinds of players?"

"Tell me, Con," I said.

"They say, 'It's not the size of the man in the fight, it's the size of the fight in the man.'"

Con Horwitz said that in praise of Detroit running back Mo Edgarson, a smallish man who had just crept a couple of yards to midfield in a rushing effort of little consequence.

Neither team had scored, and we were in the second quarter. Ted Charles, the head zebra, had, I believed, done his best to get one team or the other into the end zone. He had flung penalty flags with the determination of a soldier lobbing hand grenades, and both teams had a few first-and-goal opportunities, but they ended up with field-goal attempts that went wide or were blocked.

Just before halftime, Con Horwitz said, "It's second down for the Lions. They look ready to break this impasse, Red Crossley. You've had a chance to take an in-depth look at these two teams. How have they prepared for this contest?"

"Fundamentals, Con. Offense and defense."

"Absolutely! That's what this sport of football is really all about!"

Welcome to Con-ball, I thought. He didn't hear a word I said. He was deaf to every sound except his own voice. He had been that way since his first day in broadcasting.

"It's halftime here in Detroit. No score, so it could go either way. I'm Con Horwitz with Red Crossley. You're watching Sunday Afternoon Football on ESPN."

Con swiveled a bit in his chair, picked up his coffee mug and took a sip. "It's cold!" He looked up at Tia as she stood right behind us. "You want to do something about this?"

She nodded and produced a thermos of scalding coffee, plus creamer, sweetener and stir sticks. She topped him off, and steam rose from his mug up into his nostrils. He said nothing, but doctored up his java and sipped at it without complaint, so I supposed that was his way of thanking Tia for making him a bit more comfortable. Throughout the telecast, she would produce food, beverages and whatever else she thought we might want.

As we went into a commercial break, she said, "You're doing a terrific job, Red. Like it so far?"

"It's different from up here. I can see more."

"What else?" she asked.

"Better service. Better smells. Better all around."

"What do they say down on the field?"

I shrugged. "Mostly they swear a lot."

"What do they say?"

"Well, once we were on the goal line and I smiled at a linebacker. He said, 'Cocksucker.' I said, 'Your mother was my best teacher.'"

Tia threw back her head and howled.

"Don't worry," we heard crew member Colton Williams say in our headsets. "Red's microphone was off."

My halftime activities consisted of drinking coffee, eating hot dogs and making a couple of visits to the washroom. Things got busy a couple of minutes before halftime ended, when Tia instructed me to put my headset back on and pay close attention to the monitor.

Through my headset I heard the familiar voice of Chris Berman in the New York studio. He gushed on and on as if ESPN's newest color man—me, Red Crossley—had just singlehandedly won the War on Terror, found a vaccine *and* cure for AIDS and, during evenings and weekends, had invented a car that took in gasoline and spewed out pure oxygen. On the monitor, I watched with a grin as I, a long-legged kid in a Northup Kodiaks jersey, ran dozens of yards past a handful of defenders. Moments later, the monitor showed me as a Bayporte Invader, again eluding tacklers on my way to six points. Finally, Red Crossley appeared in a home video on the balcony of his Bayporte condominium with supermodel-turned-actress Sheri Rawson, the two of them pawing each other and making faces at the camera.

"Red, you're live with Chris," said Tia as the cameraman spun his equipment around to face me.

Looking away from the lens, I said, "Hello, Chris. We're having plenty of football fun out here in the windy, chilly Midwest."

My headset crackled with static. I frowned at Tia

Just say something, she mouthed.

"Chris," I said, "thank you for reminding the world of a few of my achievements. Unfortunately, you forgot to mention my two Nobel Prizes and how I saved the Canadian prime minister from being assassinated. But maybe you can use that for the next insert."

The second half belonged to Painless O'Neal.

Painless did little more than slap the ass of Detroit wide receiver Mickey Thome as Thome caught a screen pass and ran 20 yards for a touchdown. In his own end zone, Dreamer, hit in the numbers with the ball, bobbled it for a moment or two before batting it into the hands of a Detroit running back for a Lions touchdown. Minutes later, Painless showed everyone his speed when he and a teammate, Brock Jennings, chased Detroit wide receiver Maurice Raynes as Raynes caught a pass and ran 85 yards for a touchdown. Painless didn't catch Raynes, but he did catch, and trip, Jennings just as Jennings was about to tackle Raynes before they reached the end zone.

When not covertly helping his opponents, Painless acted like a man on crystal meth, tweaking and jumping and spitting, as if he couldn't wait for the play to start so he could bash in someone's face.

Con Horwitz loved it.

"Have you ever seen such a fierce and relentless competitor! I'll say you haven't, and you aren't likely to see another Painless O'Neal at any time in the near or distant future!"

Ted Charles kept trying to help the Giants score by repeatedly penalizing the Lions' defense for infractions real and imagined, but the Giants failed to score.

From the control truck, Ray Washburn, our producer, asked if I wanted to say something about Ted Charles.

I said I would, and my chance came soon. Charles called defensive holding against the Lions, and on the instant replay, I could see that no holding had occurred.

Into my live microphone, I said, "If Ted Charles throws any more unnecessary flags around, he's going to end up with arthritis."

I felt a tap on my shoulder. I looked up and saw Tia smiling and making an OK sign.

The last two minutes seemed the longest, as NFL broadcasts often did. The officials would call more timeouts so that the network could run more commercials while their inflated NFL audience remained.

Detroit would win this game, 28-0.

"Let Red close it out, Con," said Colton Williams.

Con said, "Well, Red Crossley, the Detroit Lions did what they needed to do today, which was to slay some Giants—Giants from the Big Apple! Detroit, home of Motown, is one of the music capitals of the world, and tonight they'll be dancing in the streets of this big, brawny burg. Those bullies from back east came out here to play a football game, but they got owned, bought and sold like a General Motors car, and taught who's boss. Those Detroit Lions look like Super Bowl contenders, if you ask me."

Tia got his attention, pointed to me, and Con said, "Red Crossley, what did *you* make of this contest today?"

"Well, Con, here's what I think: Detroit won this game today. And why did they win it? Because they scored more points. Of course, that's just *my* opinion."

TWELVE

Sneaking around has never been one of my particular talents. If I had entered the military as a spy, the bad guys would have found me immediately and I would have blabbed all the classified information they demanded to know.

So it was with my wife when I played football. Sheri had only to shoot me a sidelong glance or arch an eyebrow upon my return from a road trip with the Invaders, and I would tell her what I had been up to and with whom, even if some of those people were strippers, prostitutes or football groupies.

I amazed and scared myself, therefore, when, over the next couple of months, I started handling the Tia Gomez issue with much guile and craftiness. To the West Coast people in my life, my stage manager remained "Tino Gomez," if the matter ever came up, which it seldom did.

I had to live the life of a professional traveler, playing the part of Sheri's Westwood House husband on Monday through Wednesday, then packing a few items on Thursday morning and taking the shuttle to Los Angeles International Airport to board a flight for wherever my next game might be. I got to spend much of Thursday, all of Friday and Saturday and much of Sunday with Tia Gomez.

Did I spend more time with Tia than with my own wife? Yes—but Sheri spent more time with Sully Jackman than she did with me, her husband. If our lifestyle was wrong, the only way to make it right would have been for me to stop doing NFL games or Sheri to give up *Lally's Place*, and neither of us was the type to make major sacrifices or compromises.

I did not know who, if anyone, to blame for this peculiar situation my wife and I had gotten into. I suppose we were just a modern couple living a modern life.

After my broadcasting debut in Detroit, the network people whose opinions mattered gave me decent or better grades. Some said I should get an Emmy nomination just for being succinct and concise. A few thousand emails arrived at the network's Website, saying I was good more often than bad.

"I thought you were a badly needed breath of fresh air," Mark Richardson told me on the phone. "The only thing is, I kept waiting for you to say more. People want to hear what Red Crossley thinks of the game. I can understand why you would be reluctant to speak up, but don't be shy."

"I wasn't shy. Con Horwitz won't shut the fuck up."

Richardson laughed. "Well, so what? Talk over him. It'll work."

"Colton and Turnbull say I shouldn't do that."

"I'm the boss," he said. "Do as I say."

"Won't Con be offended if I talk while he's talking?"

"Too damn bad for Con. He's hardly the best announcer, but he's not the worst, either. He brings a certain energy that our advertisers like. "

"Really?"

"Absolutely. People love Con or they hate him, but they don't ignore him. He is highly respected for being able to talk nonstop, get into his audience's head and make people pay attention to him so that when the commercials come on, they'll pay attention to *them*."

We talked for a few more minutes, and after we hung up, I decided he was full of shit and I should get as much money for my services as I could before the network folded due to its inability to compete against Netflix and all the other alternatives to televised football games.

By the end of October, Sheri had completed two more episodes of *Lally*, and she felt they both sucked balls. Arnold Shapiro and Faith Podborsky, the two executive producers, had written both of them.

In one episode, Cesar, a handsome goof with a murky past, checks in at Lally's hotel and she is supposed to become infatuated with him.

"If Lally's going to have a crush, why must he be a goof?" Sheri asked Faith.

"Cesar is handsome, and women are attracted to handsome men."

"But he's a goof, and Lally wouldn't date a goof, even a handsome one."

Arnold came up to them and said, "Sheri, haven't you watched all the classic movies? The handsome man always gets the girl!"

"In this case," Sheri said in a voice loud enough to wake the dead, "the handsome goof rents a room and jerks off to porno movies!"

Cesar stayed in the script, but Sheri and Sully made such a commotion whenever Cesar and Lally were supposed to lock eyes and smile that Faith and Arnold changed things a bit. Since Lally's hotel was in

Los Angeles and Cesar was a spick or wetback or something, everyone agreed that she could be nice to him so he would accept a job as a busboy in Lally's coffee shop.

In the other episode, Lally agrees to see her best friend's psychiatrist and becomes smitten with him.

"Lally would never see a shrink," said Sheri.

"Why not?" asked Faith.

"Because *I* wouldn't. All shrinks do is make work for themselves. They don't teach people how to solve their own problems. They just say, 'You can't stop therapy now! You're still weird!'"

"Oh," said Faith.

...

One late morning in October, as we lay in bed in our Westwood House suite and I had a few hours before packing up and flying off to another city for a few hours, I rolled over and started asking Sheri about Sully Jackman. She told me he was British, and that his ex-wife was in London somewhere with their three children. He had been living in California for some years and considered Los Angeles his home.

"Does he have a girlfriend?" I asked my wife. "I mean, besides you."

She narrowed her eyes and stuck out her chin a bit. "What's *that* supposed to mean? We work together. We know each other."

"You eat together. A lot."

"If we didn't eat, we would starve and die." Then, "How come you leave town on Thursday when your game is on Sunday?"

"Are you accusing me of something, Sheri?"

I told her that Thursday was my travel day, and that once I reached my destination, I needed Friday and Saturday to orient myself to where I was and what I needed to do and know. I had to work with my crew on who was playing, what their strengths and weaknesses were and what, if any, postseason prospects each team had. We needed to do inserts and I needed to meet with the head coaches to say hidy and wish them well.

"The big difference between what *we* do and *you* do," I said, "was that if you don't get it right, you just do it over. In my job, it's *live*, and we don't have the luxury of saying, 'Oh, shit! That sucked balls! Let's do take two.'"

Sheri sighed. "Well, I guess there's nothing bad about our marriage that a few decades of therapy can't help."

"We have a terrific marriage, Sheri—at least compared to a few hundred other couples we know."

She giggled then, a real Sheri-style *hehehehe*, and we made out the way we had countless times before, the way we had done so rarely of late because we had allowed ambition or fate or whatever to separate us for two or three thousand miles each weekend.

In our act of intimacy, we tacitly expressed a determination *never* to let the bastards of the world, with their NFL games and sitcom pilots and hotels and flights, grind us down and destroy our love.

A few hours later, as I picked up my overnight bag and blew my wife a kiss from the doorway, she propped herself up on her pillows, turned on the TV with the handheld remote and said, "I'll see you when I see you, Bubba."

The ludicrous thing to me about my relationship with Tia Gomez was that I felt guilt even though we were friends and colleagues but absolutely, positively nothing more. I considered myself a man of some astuteness in matters of discerning a woman's interest in me, and I felt humbled, even disappointed, in how she flattered and praised me, practically pelting me with verbal roses and blinding smiles and unspoken promises of founding a Red Crossley fan club. All the while, she had given me not the slightest hint of wishing me to tear off her blouse, shake her out of her Levi's and toss her into the sack for some carnal fun.

So we had entered into a fun, frustrating buddyhood of meals, extended coffee breaks, and, most agonizing, late-morning indoor swims in whichever luxury hotel the network had booked us into. Tia splashed about in a bikini had scarcely covered her magnificent privates. Like all beautiful women, she loved teasing the men who craved her, and as I, leering and greedy, got my hands on her magnificent breasts, she slipped out of my manly grasp, stuck out her tongue and challenged me to race her the length of the pool.

I told Flash how badly I'd wanted to pull down her bikini bottoms and discover a discolored butt burn, or a huge mole sprouting hairs, that would have disgusted me into flaccidity.

Flash had already met Tia. We had sneaked off to meet up with him in Manhattan for a couple of nights.

"If you weren't so ugly, you'd really have it made," he'd said to her when I introduced them.

We drank and walked during those evenings, showing Tia the Manhattan we loved. Flash observed immediately that Tia, aside from being gorgeous, had some things in common with Sheri: Both women could function well even after half a dozen drinks, neither had any use for street drugs, both could sit around and make small talk for hours at a time, and both laughed loudly and mirthfully at things they thought funny.

Tia's closest thing to a home was the Lower East Side apartment in which she kept her clothes. Her Manhattan differed from ours; hers was an island of inexpensive ethnic restaurants of which football studs like Red and Flash knew nothing. Her studio apartment, scarcely bigger than a closet, had a pull-down bed she had to push back up in order to get to the washroom.

I knew about her minuscule apartment because she'd told me about it. She did not invite me in to see it, nor did I tell her to come check out my digs in Bayporte whenever she went there.

On our nights with Flash, the three of us did hardly anything except drink ourselves goofy and laugh at what a bitch life could be.

Tia had never stayed up drinking with us till dawn. She always checked the time and left us at around two, when taxis were relatively easy to flag down.

On one of those evenings, just as we sat in a tavern booth and watched Tia wave at and jog towards a Yellow Cab, that Flash shared some insights with me.

She'd had a long visit with us and so dominated the conversation that Flash and I just sat back and listened. Tia began to gush about Sheri. "She's too awesome. When will I meet her? I can't wait!" Flash grinned at me, and I shrugged. "She's the most beautiful woman ever to be in an ad. She's got great titties. I'm sure they're natural. A great ass, too. Not too small. A woman should have a decent-sized tush," Tia told us. "Her father is, like, the richest man in Canada. I'm sure she's just stunning in every way. That's why she got you, Red. Lucky her!

"It's such a great story," she went on, looking past us as her eyes took on a dreamy cast. "The three of you growing up together? And all three of you going on to do such big things in this world and have so much success. And you still love each other."

Tia said she had left her old friends behind. "Or they left *me* behind. I'm not sure which."

"What do you think about that?" Flash asked me after Tia had left. "She's going on and on as if Sheri were the most incredible woman alive. You better believe that she wants to fuck the man who's married to Sheri. Sure, you have money, you're a celebrity, you're an older man compared to her. She wants you, Red."

"Why me? She can have whichever man she wants."

"Exactly. She wants to prove to herself that she *can* have you. It turns her on that she can lay Sheri Rawson's husband. It's like she's saying to Sheri, 'Hey, bitch, I just laid your husband. I fucked him and made him come. How do you feel about that?'"

"Then what is Tia waiting for?" I asked him.

"Tia's saying, 'Red, what are *you* waiting for? Here I am, come and get me.'"

I shook my head. "I'm not sure I want to do that. She's a fun travel companion. If she wasn't there, I would have to listen to Con Horwitz talk about himself. Anyway, sex changes things."

"Does it?"

"Yes, it does. It means having an extramarital

affair. That's an ugly business."

"Why do you think Tia wants to have an affair? She's probably got some hot boyfriend who screws other girls," Flash said. "Her guy screws around, so does she. That happens sometimes, you know."

"If you're so eager to see her get fucked," I said with a laugh, "why don't *you* do it?"

"Maybe she don't want me."

"Every woman alive wants *you*, Flash."

He smirked. "I've already fucked my share of Tias."

"Really? You think she's like the others? I thought Tia was unique and extraordinary."

"Red, they're *all* 'unique and extraordinary.'"

Just then a Jeter Davis song started playing on the overhead sound system. We smiled and stopped talking because we felt pleased that our old friend had become popular enough to be played in New York. We also felt saddened that he had died in his prime.

Jeter had been dead a few years. As the cliché said, he had lived fast, loved hard and died young. A Bayporte native like us, he had played ball with us and attended Northup University. He decided in college to stop studying whatever crap he was majoring in and do what really turned him on, which was writing and performing music. It took him a while to find himself musically, and crowds booed him off the stage a few times, but he achieved fame as a sort of Gordon Lightfoot/Neil Young-inspired balladeer with some Joni Mitchell influences.

When the Bayporte Invaders played in the Super Bowl at home, Jeter threw a party that lasted a week and cost a scandalous amount of money. He invited celebrities, millionaires and women with big titties.

Jeter didn't believe in sleep. He thought crystal meth and crack cocaine could keep him awake indefinitely. A few times he passed out in front of me and I thought he was dead.

"What's the good of living," he wanted to know, "if you're asleep and can't enjoy nothin'?"

Jeter was only in his early thirties when his tour bus went off the freeway in northwestern Washington state and plunged into the valley below. Nobody was ever sure of why the bus went off the road. Maybe Jeter insisted on driving and fell asleep at the wheel.

When his song ended, I said to Flash, "Maybe I'll just do my usual thing about Tia—nothing. If she wants to throw me into the backseat and have her way with me, well, I'll just think that it was meant to happen."

"Or you can just do it, like I said. If you don't, you'll just make yourself bonkers. Just treat her the way Phil Ruble treats his bimbos like Suzy Boobies."

"You mean just say, 'Hey, Tia, wanna fuck?'"

Flash laughed. "It's been known to work."

THIRTEEN

Dreadful news came from Bayporte in December. Rickey Robinson reported that his brother Scoliosis had become a follower of a holy man who was contemptuous of football, and L.T. Briggs had flown into a panic over what to do about it.

L.T. and Lord Larry had assumed that Scoliosis had made a commitment to play for the Northup University Kodiaks, and felt horrified by Rickey's announcement that a spiritual guru named Bhagwan Ram Dass had persuaded Scoliosis to renounce football altogether and spend the rest of his life in India, humming and chanting and doing not much else.

"Bag one run dash? Never heard of him," I muttered. L.T. had called me at three in the morning as I lay in my bed at Westwood House.

"Neither have I, but he's out there and he's trying to steal that spade from me," L.T. said. He begged me to fly up to Bayporte immediately for an emergency meeting with Lord Larry and Rickey Robinson.

"Flash is already on his way out here, Red," he said.

I yawned. "OK, L.T., I'll do it. Gotta go up your way to cover a game, anyway."

When I reached Bayporte and entered my condominium, I called L.T. and he told me more about the Scoliosis crisis.

Due to Bhagwan's disdain for football, Scoliosis had refused to play in his high school's final game against Gosheau High. Bhagwan had visited Scoliosis' high school and given the students a talk. Since

Scoliosis was the student-body president, Bhagwan invited the young man to a private prayer session, and from that point on the athletic superstar would only mumble to himself. At game time, he just sat on the bench.

Ernie Tremont, Scoliosis' football coach, wheedled and pleaded for him to get up and play. But Scoliosis simply said, "Why play football? Why live life?"

Rickey interceded, reminding Scoliosis that he owed it to his teammates to help them destroy Gosheau High.

"Why those nice boys be harmin' each other?" Scoliosis replied. "I just wants to love all people."

"Big money's at stake here, guy," Rickey said.

"Bhagwan say money have no spiritual value. He say happiness don't come from what's on the scoreboard."

"Yeah, well, Bhagwan be smokin' the wrong kind of shit," Rickey said. "Go out there and kick some Gosheau ass!"

Nothing doing. Scoliosis would not play, ever. He wanted only to eat plants and think pure thoughts.

Neither L.T. nor Lord Larry had actually met Bhagwan. Rickey, their liaison, thought an economic arrangement might be in order. For adequate compensation, Bhagwan would try to persuade Scoliosis to play football again.

"I'm not sure holy men take bribes," L.T. said. "Don't it suck balls, Red? I found the next great thing in college football and now some Paki weirdo is playin' head games with him. What does that tell you about the fuckin' world we live in?"

"What's going on with DeShonn Jones? Any

problems there?"

"No, everything's all right. He's ready to put on that brown-and-gold jersey and make Kodiaks history. The only thing is, we have to guarantee him that he'll get to play as much as Scoliosis does, but I'm OK with that."

"Sounds good," I said.

"But I just can't get over how bad this Scoliosis thing has gotten. Tell me how some dumbass Paki con man could get a spade football stud to start worryin' about 'existential' shit!"

"Sounds like you need to get into a huddle with your friends and figure this out," I told him. "Flash and I will meet up with you in Lord Larry's office as soon as possible."

"Red, I'll be straight with you," L.T. said. "I feel like someone's pissed on my corn flakes and force-fed 'em to me!"

With just a week left in the regular season, things were working out very well for Painless O'Neal and the NFL Players' Association. Virtually all teams had compiled the worst, or at least mediocre, records in recent memory.

Painless boasted to me that the Players' Association had become stronger than ever.

"Everybody is playing half-assed football, Red, so it's wide open. Every team has a chance to make the postseason," he'd said.

The Commissioner, uncertain of what else to say or do, gave the issue the same spin as Painless: Parity was a good thing; even the worst team might make go all the way and its long-suffering fans might finally have bragging rights.

But sportswriters smelled bullshit and said as much.

Phil Ruble wrote in his online column, "What would I rather do than watch an NFL game? I'll tell you: Buy a condo in Afghanistan; attend a Britney Spears concert; sit through a Keanu Reeves film festival; become a Scientologist; get married again."

I flipped through my wall calendar and updated it to December. Such a family-oriented time of year. Looking around at my big, handsome condo, I had to remind myself that this was *my* home, even if I hadn't felt *at* home here in some time. My wife lived out of a suitcase in Los Angeles, or maybe crashed at Sully Jackman's house some nights, and might never return to our apartment. She had decorated the place with heavy sofas of fine leather, Oriental rugs and several loathsome pieces of Jackson Pollock abstract art that she loved.

Flash, truly devoted to writing and mostly a New Yorker by now, still owned a third of our condo and had left behind some of his books and clothing. Although indigent compared to Sheri, he had enough money to last a few lifetimes and seemed content enough to stay in Manhattan and do his writing; but inevitably I expected him broach the subject of his equity in our Bayporte residence and inquire if we wished to buy him out—and, if so, for how much?

Such a question depressed me, not because of the money involved; Sheri, if it came to that, would take less than two minutes to negotiate a fair price and hand him a cashier's check later that day. I dreaded that. Flash's sale of his share to us would mean to me the end of our deliciously youthful and naughty roommate arrangement, a *menage a trois* in which the girl had screwed her boys many times, always separately but, occasionally, doing one while the other watched and masturbated.

Flash had moved on; I resented him. I wanted us to stay together forever, so we could return to being three kids playing house, refusing to grow up.

Oh well.

I knew he wanted to meet with me at Pandora's Box, so I showered and shaved, then called Sheri to tell her that I was back in our condo and that terrorists hadn't crashed the plane into the Rawson Enterprises building or anything.

I dialed her number, and a woman with an Asian accent answered.

"Is this Sheri?" I asked.

"This is Twee."

"Where is Sheri?"

"No Sheri here."

"Where is Sheri? Sheri Rawson. Sheri Crossley. This is her husband. You're holding her phone."

"Oh, Cherry! Cherry on tennis court. Busy playing with Mister Sully."

"Tell her not to squeeze his balls too hard," I said.

Pandora's Box was full of men trying to get laid and women trying to get paid. I struggled through the bar and said hidy to Flash and Phil Ruble, who had cleared out some room for themselves. Flash shook my hand and said, "Order us another round, Red. I'm gonna go see what those girls want for Christmas."

Moments after I had ordered my first Canadian

Comfort over ice, Phil started working the room. He went up to a lovely young blonde with big natural zoomers. Her T-shirt said PLEASE KEEP YOUR EYES ON THE ROAD.

"Excuse me!" Phil said, grabbing the blonde by her upper arm. "Do you speak English?"

"What country do you think this is?"

"I'm Phil Ruble. Who you?"

"I'm someone who is not interested in you," she said.

Phil stared at her breasts. "What's that say on your shirt? I'm dyslexic or illiterate or something."

"It says that if you can't read the shirt, you can't afford the goodies inside of it."

"Want me to buy you a drink?" he asked.

"Thanks, but I already have one."

"Then do you want to meet my famous friends over there?"

She waved in our direction. "Hiya, guys."

Flash and I waved back. "We're retired Invaders," I said.

"Oh," she said, "did you invade Iraq or Afghanistan?"

"No, Invaders with a capital I. Bayporte Invaders football team," I said.

"Got too old to play, eh?" she said.

"Something like that," I said.

"Gotta go. See ya." She disappeared into the crowd.

"Doncha love mingling with the common folk?" I asked Flash.

"I'm just having too much fun," he replied.

A few hours later, the three of us stood outside Good Girls, reading the marquee and feeling pleased that Suzy Boobies would be performing.

We went inside, paid twenty dollars each and had our hands stamped by a scowling bouncer who probably hadn't had a chance to manhandle anyone all night.

On stage, heavy metal music blared as Suzy Boobies fondled a big white plastic cross as if it were someone's big dick. We groped our way through the darkness to the bar as Suzy Boobies stripped down to her birthday suit and played with herself.

"I thought church girls weren't supposed to do that," Flash said.

We ordered enough Canadian Comfort to keep us warm through a Yukon winter as we watched Suzy celebrate her faith. Once our eyes adjusted to the darkness, we surveyed the audience.

"There he is," Flash said. "There's Ted Charles."

I looked to where Flash pointed. "Damn, you're right." Seeing Ted Charles in Good Girls made me feel better about Flash's *Playboy* article. I now believed that the official had some sort of relationship with the stripper.

I had just enough Canadian Comfort in my veins to want to over and say hello to Charles.

"Do it," Flash said. "I'd love to know his reaction."

I took a Canadian Comfort over ice with me to Ted's table and sat down uninvited.

"How's it goin', eh? Remember me, Ted?"

"Red Crossley! Didn't expect to see you in here!" he said.

"I didn't know you were a patron of the live erotic

performing arts."

He introduced me to his friends. "Amnon, Clark, Steve—meet Red Crossley. Red, these guys are here for a convention in Bayporte."

His friends were from Alberta, and he thought he should show them some Bayporte nightlife. Ted believed that Bayporte was much more fun than most people thought. He added that they were about to leave so they could check out some other Bayporte nightclubs.

"You've made a good start on your second career, Red," Ted told me. "I've never heard you because I'm on the field while you're up in the booth, but I'm told you're becoming a good announcer. You get to the point and you know when to shut up."

Clark pointed to the stage and we watched as Suzy spread her legs and showed us what God had given her. The song had changed to some guitar-based noise that seemed to be called "More Human Than Human."

When Suzy closed her legs, I leaned over and said to Ted, "I know you don't like to talk to broadcasters, but mind if I ask you a question?"

"Red," he replied, "*I* don't mind, but the NFL gets uptight about it when we talk to you guys."

"Just one question. I won't ask again."

Ted sipped his beer and shrugged. "Ask."

"Why do *you* throw so many fuckin' flags, guy?"

He winced and sipped some more beer. "Ha! I *knew* you would ask me that."

Ted's friends paid us no mind. Suzy had started showing us her vag again.

"Red," Ted said, "I'll be very honest with you. Nobody knows how hard we work. *Nobody*. I work harder than most, and I throw the flags whenever I see an infraction. That makes me unpopular, but who cares? I keep a clear conscience."

Officials in NFL games were referees, umpires, field judges, head linesman and back judges. The referee was always the boss, and Ted Charles was always the referee.

Ted, like most others in his line of work, had gone into officiating as a hobby while his current career thrived. He'd started out as a college zebra and kept quiet about his aspirations to work NFL games.

The NFL would watch him work college games for a couple of seasons, and if he did more good than bad, they would evaluate his physical fitness and vision, plus a test to see if he understood NFL rules.

The league required zebras to pass the eye test every years. Flash wondered if Ted bribed the league to let it slide.

"Ted is the boss out there," Flash had said, "and he works with the same crew, and they know he has the power to overrule their flags. If one of them wants to sneeze, he'll say, 'Let me check with Ted to make sure it's OK.' He's worse than Caligula out there.

"I can't prove that Ted and his crew are fixing games, but I still think they're doing that. They get their game assignments with plenty of time to tell their friends and acquaintances which teams are 'looking good.'

"The league tells the zebras to keep their games assignments a secret so that Vegas and Osama bin Laden and so on can't call the officials in the middle of the night and say, 'You better make sure my team wins or else.'

"But if the zebras are so fucking conscientious about keeping secrets, how come Uncle Rex and the hotel valets in Vegas know where Ted Charles is working every Sunday?"

I sipped on my Canadian Comfort over ice and leaned over to Ted Charles as Suzy jiggled her boobies for our viewing pleasure.

"Ted, you *know* how many people are skeptical of your refereeing. All those flags at the most crucial times! What's up with that?"

"I call 'em as I see 'em," he replied. "Do I miss some? Probably, but at the time I thought they were right. Am I going to apologize to you or anyone else? No. Maybe the NFL should have a new policy in which they scrutinize every instant replay in which I throw a flag. It would make football boring as hell, though."

I finished my drink and said, "Ted, are you aware that every high- and low-roller in Vegas and Atlantic City thinks you fix games?"

"Red, did you know that I can't help what people think? If they think I'm crooked, that's not my problem." Then, "I don't fix games, Red. I don't throw passes or make touchdowns. I just toss flags when the players try to cheat."

I got up and nodded at Ted's friends. "Pleasure to meet you."

They glanced in my direction, then looked again at Suzy, whose vag was wide open again.

I returned to the bar and said to Flash, "Ted certainly has plenty to say about his officiating."

"So does Suzy."

Suzy closed her legs, smiled at the audience and disappeared. So did Ted and his friends.

After close to an hour, Suzy came out in a black T-shirt, black Levi's and black boots. She saw Flash and me at the bar and came running up to us. Phil Ruble stood next to us, talking to his young friend Patti.

"You *guys!*" Suzy said after the third or fourth hug. "Let me say thanks that you've come back to say hi." She put her hands together and muttered for a few moments.

Then she jumped around a bit and added, "Did I tell you two what happened? *Playboy* sent a staff photographer up here to *shoot* me for the issue that has Flash's piece!"

"Does Ted come in here much?" Flash asked.

Suzy rolled her eyes. "Only as often as he can, which is a lot. We had a little chat in his car. I was like, 'When are you working again?' and he was like, 'I don't know yet.' So I was like, 'Well, let *know*, because there's this *rad* condo I want to buy not far from Northup, but I need one more game to afford the down payment.'"

"Going to stay put in Bayporte, eh?" I asked her.

She nodded. "It's what He wants."

"How's the career going?" Flash asked.

"Awesome!" She jumped some more. "That *Playboy* photographer? He thinks I could interest Larry Flynt because I masturbate with a crucifix, and when your article comes out, Good Girls will get so much publicity! I'll be able to triple my fee!" Then, "Look, I have two more sets here. Wanna hang out later?"

"Wish we could," I said. "But this was a very special and unexpected trip. Friend of ours needs some help, then we're gone again. I'm sort of homeless for the moment and Flash here spends most of his time in New York now. We have a meeting downtown, then we're both flying out."

"Too bad," she said. "We could party."

"Next time we're here, we'll call you," said Flash.

"Promise?" Suzy asked. "Look, I have a girlfriend here who could join us."

"I'm sure she's lovely," I said.

"Oh, she's got a rude mouth, but I'm trying to get some religion into her, and no one's ever complained about her capacity to love."

"Suzy, we really must go," Flash said.

"This is on me," she said, grabbing our bar bill and stuffing it between her big breasts.

"We're leaving," I said to Phil. "Coming?"

"No," he said. "But I want you to meet Patti." The girl was about nineteen, blonde and slim, sort of a trashy version of a Northup cheerleader.

Patti rummaged through her purse, produced a capsule of some kind and swallowed it with a mouthful of vodka.

Phil chuckled. "This girl is nineteen but has the emotional development of a six-year-old."

"Why don't you sit on my face?" she asked him.

Phil burst out laughing and clutched his heart. "Quick, someone get me some nitroglycerin!"

Flash and I waved goodnight and headed out to eat some breakfast and talk about a man they called Bhagwan.

FOURTEEN

Through the huge glass walls of Lord Larry's thirtieth-floor office in the Rawson Enterprises building, one could see virtually everything worth seeing in Bayporte.

On the two mahogany-paneled walls, Lord Larry had hung pictures of the mining equipment his company had used over the years to bring scandalous wealth to its boss.

Some of that mining equipment had belonged to "Black Eye" Rawson, the grandfather Sheri had never met. "Black Eye," a randy Newfoundlander, had migrated to Great Elizabeth in search of gold, silver and platinum. What he found instead was coal—tons of it, thus his nickname.

Sheri's grandpa had given Lord Larry a good start in life by paying his Northup tuition, buying him an Edsel and keeping his pocket full of walking-around money. To Lord Larry's credit, he expanded and diversified the company in ways "Black Eye" wasn't smart enough to know about.

Lord Larry, who had lettered as a Kodiak—at six-three and 200 hundred pounds, he was big enough to be a cornerback—distinguished himself as being more than a well-off student with a deep voice and a Canadian brogue he liked to exaggerate when speaking to conceited Americans. He graduated as a geology major and, three years later, received a law degree from Northup.

He started mining for things other than coal. One of the things he found in Bayporte was Joy Marie Hakola, a pretty, sweet-natured girl from a nothing family.

In the early 'Sixties, Sheri Lynn Rawson was born. Her dad was handsome and her mum pretty; they knew their little girl would become someone special. The only thing I couldn't understand was why Sheri had no siblings. Hadn't Lord Larry, deep down inside, wanted a son to carry on his name?

Around this time, Lord Larry mining crews found huge deposits of zinc, molybdenum and, of course, coal, everywhere they looked throughout Great Elizabeth. Then he made major strikes in other provinces, in half a dozen American states, and overseas. He took up sailing, golf and flying; he became a demonic tennis player. Maybe that was why he settled on having just one child—he had too many hobbies and saw little attraction in the daily tedium of childrearing. Still, like most other rich men, he would simply hired nannies to raise his offspring.

Lord Larry loved Canada, Great Elizabeth and Bayporte, his family and friends, and his company. He had no use at all for anyone who felt otherwise.

"Red," he had told me, "I say what I think, and do as I please. If anyone doesn't like it, they can kiss my ass."

The Larry Rawsons were as close to being Canadian royalty was one could be—he through birth and achievement, and his wife through having the good sense to marry him.

That morning, as I sat in his office, I heard Lord Larry mutter something about wanting Bhagwan Dass Ram killed. Did anyone have the phone number of a hit man...?

Lord Larry, L.T. Briggs, Rickey, Flash and I sat at the table in the conference room, guzzling premium imported coffee and staring at Lord Larry.

"You think I'm bullshittin'?" he asked us. "You think I can't put a contract on this clown? I know people in Vegas and Atlantic City! I can get that bastard blown to nirvana and I wouldn't have no conscience about it! Overseas assholes piss me off enough when they come over in their fancy suits and tell me how to do my business. But now I have a crazy Paki who's diddling around with Northup University football! Shitfuck!"

"India is a bloody joke," said L.T. "It's got a billion people and they all want to come here and get jobs at McDonald's."

"I'm not sure killing that holy man is the way to go," said Flash. "I think we need the holy man to help Scoliosis get mentally together."

Rickey nodded. "Bhagwan doesn't mess around. Mister Larry authorized me to offer the holy man half a mil to help Scoliosis, but the holy man just closed his eyes and started chanting."

That half-million dollars made quite an impression on me. So did Rickey. Like most other successful people, he became whoever he needed to be, in order to make things go his way. He talked that "dumb nigger" stuff because he knew some people expected it. But Rickey was smart and savvy—he had an astute glint in his eye that most people didn't bother to look for, so they assumed he was stupid and their inaccurate appraisal allowed him to exploit and manipulate them. He had played football at Louisiana State and earned a business degree. Before becoming Lord Larry's "assistant," Rickey had been the accountant for Chicken Bicken, a fast-food chain throughout Louisiana and Alabama.

Rickey, son of a manual laborer, had gone to college and then taken the accounting job as a means of escaping rural Louisiana. Now he aimed for even bigger things through his kid brother.

"Larry," I said to my father-in-law, "would you really consider paying that much money for Scoliosis?"

"To get the Kodiaks a national title? Damn right," he replied. "In fact, I would pay even more. If we get him and that Jones boy, we'll be King Shit of Canadian college football."

"I don't think Bhagwan cares about money," Rickey told us. "That's not where his soul is at. He believes that money cannot buy happiness."

"That so?" asked L.T. "Sure sounds like the guy is after whatever money *can* buy."

"And the guy sure wants a lot of that awful money that corrupts us all," Flash said.

Lord Larry sighed. "I will go as high as one million dollars. But I would need absolute assurance that Scoliosis is all set and ready to go, not staring at his belly button all day."

"Staring at *what?*" I asked, looking over at Rickey.

"Scoliosis spends every morning in deep mediation and contemplation," Rickey said. "Sometimes he does some navel-gazing. He says he can see an entire universe down there."

"I don't want to hear about any more about belly buttons and meditating," L.T. said. "The only thing I'm concerned about is that the best player we could ever have is wasting his time down there in Louisiana and we need to get him back up here."

Lord Larry said, "I have a plan. Red, you and Flash go down there to see Scoliosis. See where his head is at and if he'll listen to reason. You're a couple of famous ex-footballers and maybe he has some respect for you."

If we failed with Scoliosis, we could get a meeting with the holy man and offer him a million dollars to make Scoliosis believe that the path to spiritual enlightenment led straight through Northup University. Bhagwan could take all the money at once or arrange some sort of payment plan, if the great man really cared enough about money to make specific financial arrangements.

"A million is the best I can do," Lord Larry said. "It's up to the holy man to accept it or reject it."

Rickey nodded. "Give me a day or so to contact Bhagwan and get the meeting scheduled. He doesn't live in Merde; he'll have to travel from Baton Rouge."

"I've done all I can," Lord Larry said, sitting back in his chair and running a hand through his hair. "If my plan fails, we'll just have to find another spade who can run like the wind."

"I have a good feeling about your plan," Rickey told Lord Larry. "A million dollars can be very persuasive. I'm sure Bhagwan will understand very well where you're coming from."

Flash's article on the NFL appeared in the latest edition of *Playboy*, so we bought a couple of copies in the Marriott's gift shop after checking in. We turned off our smart phones and ordered room-service meals.

The first call I took came from Sheri.

"Tell Flash I've just finished reading his *Playboy*

article. The cashier looked at me a little weird when I bought the magazine, but I told him I get off on looking at pictures of naked women." She laughed. "But seriously, that article is the classic 'Everyman abused by the flag-throwing zebras' conflict."

"You sound exhausted."

"I've been playing tennis with Sully. His court is beautiful, and so is the rest of his house."

"How's *Lally*?"

"It's improving, and so is morale. And that's freaking us out. What if we're a hit? What if we get nominated for Emmys?"

"I hear I'm going to be nominated, too," I told her.

"Sweet. Anyway, Arnold and Faith are lightening up a bit and each day is better. We have time to relax and unwind a bit."

"Well," I said, "I suppose that's a good thing."

"You know what, Red? These positive changes have happened in the past day or two. Sully says show business works that way: A quality project brings people together and sorts out its own problems. It overcomes its own inertia and generates its own torque."

"Sully sounds like a smart fellow."

"He plays some bitchin' tennis, too. We all hang out here now. I'm talking to you in between bites of barbecued ribs. Too yummy."

"Is it just you and him there? I can't hear any laughter or splashing around in the background. Maybe it's just these cell phones. Narrow bandwidth, you know. Poor reception."

"Sasha's here but she's in the Jacuzzi. We're expecting some other people to drop by soon. Phone reception's OK. It's just that I'm eating these ribs while we talk." I could her lips smack.

Sheri finished her food and said she regretted that I wouldn't be in Los Angeles that weekend, but maybe it was just as well—we wouldn't have much quality time together because she was so busy with *Lally*.

"I would be no fun, Red. I would just come back to our room, flop into bed and snooze away till my alarm clock went off."

"I hear ya, baby. We'll get together whenever and wherever we can. But the meantime make sure you keep your priorities straight and get a great suntan at Sully's place. Maybe even keep that beautiful body in shape by swimming in his pool.

"Just don't swim nude at his place," I admonished her. "We wouldn't want Sully to get a hard-on, right?"

Click.

Flash received a call from Painless O'Neal, saying that everyone in the NFL Players' Association was proud of Flash and his *Playboy* article.

Then Phil Ruble called, congratulating Flash on that article. Including that picture of Suzy Boobies didn't hurt Flash's chances of publishing with *Playboy*, Phil told him. The magazine had run the picture in a tactful way, with Suzy from the breasts up, her 38-inch zoomers looking firm and delectable.

He also believed that the picture of Suzy and her boobies would make Ted Charles the most envied man in the NFL.

Minutes later, Tia called, breathless. "Red, I need to locate Flash Gortton immediately. Mark Richardson wants you to interview Flash next week in Seattle. Please, do you have *any* idea at all of how to contact Flash? We'll fly him out to Seattle and pay all of his expenses. Mark is totally banging his head against the wall over this."

I held out my iPhone in Flash's direction and said, "Flash, do you want to go to Seattle with me and be interviewed for ESPN?"

"Sounds good to me," he replied in his deep, unmistakable voice.

"Oh my God!" Tia exclaimed. "You've got him there with you! And he wants to do this Seattle thing! Yea!"

"But don't tell Mark," I said. "Not yet."

"Why not?"

"Because it will look much better for you if your boss thinks Flash is somewhere in Timbuktu but you got him to go to Seattle as a special favor because of your friendship with me and my friendship with him."

"Red! You're such a sweetie! I owe you a great big kiss!"

"See you on Friday."

Tia squealed. "I've never even *been* to Seattle!"

After we hung up, I told Flash, "Part of the satisfaction of being powerful in this world comes from being able to help ambitious youngsters like Tia Gomez."

Flash poured us a couple of Canadian Comforts over ice. "Red, you better fuck that girl in Seattle. She needs to be fucked by a powerful man. If you don't, I'll happy to do the deed."

Flash's article featured a beautiful two-page illustration of a football field upon which a zebra was raising his arms to signal a touchdown as an Oakland

Raider entered the end zone. I sat up in bed and read some of it.

IF YOU CAN'T PLAY FAIR, PLAY FOOTBALL
by Wilbert "Flash" Gortton

For many years, professional football provided fun and excitement to millions of people who weren't exactly millionaires for several months of every fall.

I know about this because I played the game for a number of years and many people came up to me to tell me how much football meant to them. I left the game and good riddance. It has turned into a joke, but nobody's laughing.

Today, everywhere you look, the NFL's power positions are held by vampires.

The owners are Nazis. The general managers are as heartless as the Grim Reaper. The coaches should be injected full of medication as put somewhere so they don't hurt themselves (or anyone else). The zebras—the officials—should be shot dead and have their heads mounted on someone's wall.

They players are all grateful just to have jobs, but I'm not sure how long they, or the NFL, will last.

It's nearly time for the playoffs to begin, and I'm eager to see how those zebras will make huge money off the postseason.

They know that on virtually every play each team commits some sort of infraction, and the zebras call, or don't call, penalties as a way of controlling the game's progress and outcome. Even the honest zebras are under pressure to throw markers and keep things as close as possible so the TV viewers won't change the channel.

My favorite corrupt zebra, Ted Charles, has a stripper girlfriend whose face and breasts are below the illustration in this article.

Over the course of three years, I watched Ted Charles at work, throwing flags onto the field as freely as a fry cook tosses meat patties onto a grill.

Ted, upon being assigned games, decided which team he wanted to win and bet accordingly. Then, on game day, he did his best to make things easy and good for his team.

As the old saying goes, every opponent on the football field is formidable, but the one who's really tough to beat is wearing a striped shirt.

Earlier this season, Ted made the mistake of fixing a game as a favor to someone I knew—the aforementioned stripper. Her name is Suzy Boobies, and she performs at Good Girls, a nightclub near Bayporte, Great Elizabeth.

One night, after sex, she told me about Ted Charles' unethical behind-the-scenes activities. She didn't know that I had starting writing for a living; she thought I was still in football in some capacity who, like a greedy, sneaky stock trader, would like to exploit her "inside information."

Suzy bet on the game Ted had given her and won enough money to buy a new sports car. She told me that he assured her "there's more where that came from."

I have her sworn affidavit regarding this matter as well as her voice on a recording. Why is she cooperating with me? Well, it's not because her conscience tells her it's the right thing to.

Suzy wants international publicity because she

believes it will help her professionally. As the saying goes, there is no such thing as bad publicity, especially when you're a stripper.

If you're ever in the Greater Bayporte Area, check her out at Good Girls. You'll find out soon enough why Ted Charles gave her those football games.

Flash went on about how Ted Charles would likely respond to what he'd written. Ted could always say, quite truthfully, that on every play a penalty occurred and that he simply did his job when he threw those flags after witnessing flagrant infractions.

Also, who would believe anything said by someone who called herself "Suzy Boobies" and degraded herself for a living? Moreover, what about Flash himself? Would people take seriously allegations made by a hard-partying ex-footballer who had little to lose by kissing and telling?

NFL Commissioner Gabe Roder would respond by repeating that zebras, like top-secret government agencies, often receive criticism from writers and other negative people. Zebras, like government spies, never condescend to commenting on such criticism.

The *Playboy* lawyers and editors got nervous about Flash's article. Fearing lawsuits, they agonized over every word of it. The editors carved it up with blue pencils, while the lawyers went to work on it with their red pens. Soon the piece looked like some college freshman's half-assed term paper after a professor had gotten done with it.

After much haggling between Flash and the magazine's editorial and legal goons, Flash agreed to sign a form stating that he would take full legal responsibility for every word in his article.

Playboy ultimately ran the piece despite their nervous lawyers, who wanted to kill it altogether.

"Don't worry," Flash told the legal eagles. "My source is unassailable."

"Your source," they retorted, "is a stripper named Suzy Boobies."

"Yeah. Ain't journalism terrific?"

I could scarcely glance at my iPad without seeing something about Flash's story or the world's reaction to it. EX-STAR TACKLES NFL, REFS or something to that effect appeared on practically every online news service in North America.

They quoted Ted Charles as saying, "I don't know what Gortton wrote because my family and I don't read magazines like *Playboy*. Furthermore, I don't believe I've ever met anyone named 'Suzy Boobies.'"

To which Suzy Boobies replied, "He knows me perfectly well, and I know him. Ask him to drop his pants and I know you'll find an oval-shaped birthmark on his joint."

Matt Stevens, a cornerback for the 49ers and head of the Players' Association, said, "Ours is a free society, and therefore Flash Gortton has every right to express his views in a public forum such as a magazine. We, the Players' Association, have no knowledge of the corruption Gortton writes about, but he is entitled to write what he believes is the truth."

NFL Commissioner Gabe Roder said in a statement, "The NFL is the best it has ever been. More people than ever are going to games, wearing team apparel and tuning into games broadcast on TV, radio or online. Need I say more?"

The NFL owners, in unison, said in effect, "Flash Gortton is an idiot."

Jack Piros said, "Flash is a world-class moaner. He would decline a quickie with Cameron Diaz if he saw a zit on her nose."

When I knocked on his door the next morning, I caught Flash in the living room, laughing as he hung up his smart phone. "That was Roder."

"The commish? Why did he call you?"

"Just to tell me he liked what I had written. He couldn't say so publicly, of course, but he knew that what I had written was the truth. He knew the players were up to something naughty like a strike. He wants to wants to lean on the owners to budge on some of the issues."

Flash shook his head and laughed some more. "Gabe says Ted will be fired after this season along with a half-dozen other officials. They'll all 'retire for personal reasons.' Everyone will save face. He's been wanting to get rid of those zebras for some time now, but really didn't have anything to use as a threat. Now he does—my article. He can press charges against them if they refuse to retire."

"Chalk one up for Flash," I said.

"Gabe says he and I oughta get drunk together like we did years ago. He said he can tell me all kinds of shit about the NFL that would totally freak me out."

"He say anything else about the players, coaches and zebras?"

Flash shrugged. "He empathizes with the players, but the owners pay his on-the-job expenses."

"Life's a bitch, eh?"

FIFTEEN

We took our time driving to Merde. Neither of us had been through Louisiana, so we put the rented Honda on cruise control and didn't pay much attention to the drivers behind us who honked their horns and yelled obscenities at us before passing us on the inside.

We got thirsty, pulled into a grocery store and bought a six-pack of Budweiser tall cans, which we drank in the car. We talked about being youngsters at Oliver Johnson High School, playing Friday-night high school football games, going joyriding and having car races. Luck, and luck alone, prevented us from getting killed on those occasions. We laughed about verbal and physical brawls, girls' undies left in the backseats of cars, of contraception neglected and pregnancies aborted, of the oversized cheeseburgers and fried chicken they stopped making a long time ago.

As always, we spoke of the girls we had known, the girls we wished we had known, those who had surely gotten fat and those who had stayed slim and sexy. We remembered those who had entered early middle age as mad as hell because the dentists, lawyers or accountants they had married weren't doing enough business to buy them the West Shore houses they coveted.

Flash swore he would never have married Sheri despite their very informal engagement, though I knew he was wrong. Since ending his romance with Sheri, he hadn't been close to marrying anyone, though he got more ass than a toilet seat.

"I don't suppose I'll ever marry now," he said between sips of beer and belches in the car. "I'm feeling pretty selfish these days, Red."

"Aren't we all."

Flash shook his head. "I don't know how you married men put up with your wives. If I had married Sheri and she got on the rag, I think I'd turn her teeth upside down."

"Sheri doesn't throw things or try to kick you in the balls. She just yells and screams."

"You knew my family, Red."

Yes. Flash's mother was talking about the mental abuse his had inflicted on his father throughout Flash's childhood.

Their family owned Gortton's Groceries, a store that sold many things. Both parents and their son worked at the store. Flash, even then conscientious about football practice, received much support from his parents because they knew he had enough talent to go pro. Their store made the Gorttons a comfortable living but nothing more. They worked hard and put some money in the bank, but Mum Gortton seemed to want a better life than that, and Flash believed her dissatisfaction to be the source of her anger.

Sheri and I had never thought of Flash's mum as being angry. Demanding and stern, certainly, but always a polite lady around us.

Flash had said, "You don't know Mum like my dad and I do." His dad, a friendly man, full of smiles and waves, acted as if running a corner store were the fulfillment of a lifelong dream. If Flash's assessment of his mother was accurate, I had to wonder why Dad Gortton smiled all the time.

In their apartment upstairs from the store, Mum Gortton felt compelled to tell her husband and son what to wear, eat, say and watch on TV; where to sit; what to buy and how much money to spend; how cool or warm to keep the room; why they must not have a dog, cat or bird; where, when and for how long they should go on vacation; which movies to see or miss; who was worthy of their friendship or not; and virtually all other matters that arose in everyday life.

If Flash and Dad Gortton ever disputed her wisdom, Mum would likely make her two fellows regret having been born.

When Flash, Sheri and I were seniors at Oliver Johnson High School, Mum Gortton died. She'd been struck by a car while jaywalking. The paramedics scraped her off the roadway and delivered her to Bayporte General Hospital. Flash had virtually camped out at her bedside while the doctors tried to stabilize her, but her internal injuries were too severe and she died, asleep, while her son spoke to her of their good times together.

Mum Gortton had some hours of consciousness, even lucidity, during which he bossed everyone around. Knowing that her death was imminent, she told Flash and Dad Gortton that she wanted to be buried in her blue dress from Nolan, the upscale retailer. Brice from Nolan's downstairs salon should do her hair, though he was frightfully expensive. She wanted them to play Barbra Streisand's greatest hits during her service. Mum Gortton's wishes were modest compared to those of Carol Cox, a coed we had known at Northup. Carol, the ungainly daughter of a rich seafood canner, became a diabetic through her compulsive consumption of Canada Dry ginger ale. She died after a five-day binge of the stuff. After being warned by her endocrinologist that such an addiction might be imminently fatal, Carol told her father she wanted to be buried in her best Bill Blass dress, sitting in her Miata, surrounded by bottles of Canada Dry.

Less than a year after his mum died, Flash got a stepmum. Dad Gortton married Fannie Hollister, the sales representative who always came in to see if they needed any more snack foods. Later on, after Flash, Sheri and I students at Northup University, Dad Gortton sold the grocery store at a large enough profit to retire.

Dad Gortton and Fannie, a woman Flash found much easier to be around than his mother, bought a winter home in Arizona. Flash would go out there sometimes to visit them, and would stay until he could no longer bear their company and conversation.

Now entering middle age, and mostly a resident of New York City, Flash spoke with humor of his Bayporte years. He laughed aloud as he recalled the time Mum Gortton went red with resentment at one of Dad Gortton's offhand remarks, then punished Dad *and* Flash with weeks of stony silence over that most innocent of observations.

At the dinner table, what Dad Gortton had said was, "My mum used to cook with butter instead of margarine. I guess that's why everything was always so yummy."

Now, as we drove towards Merde, we went past one sleepy, happy town after another.

"Looks nice and peaceful, hey?" Flash said. "Do you know what's happening inside those houses?"

"Temper tantrums and hurt feelings?"

"Fucking right. But I always ask myself, 'Why do people fight? Why can't they just get along?'"

"If you ever figure it out," I told him, "tell me."

"There are times," he said with a sigh, "when I actually feel lonely. And that's a new thing for me. I can be with some gorgeous naked woman who's doing her best to make me feel good, and all I feel is lonely."

"Then get married," I told him.

"Not *that* lonely."

We both laughed.

"I think I'm going to start on a new novel," he said. "For inspiration, I think I'll get a young housekeeper who can do massages."

"A live-in housekeeper?"

He nodded. "Someone who looks like Tia Gomez and doesn't speak English."

"If she doesn't speak English," I asked, "how are you going to make friends with her and overcome your loneliness?"

"I don't want her friendship," he said. "I already have enough friends, and I'm going to put all of them—and you—in my novel."

We met up with Scoliosis Robinson and his coach, Ernie Tremont, at Al's Restaurant in downtown Merde.

The downtown, if one could call it that, was a courthouse surrounded by half a dozen boarded-up storefronts. In front of the restaurant were a few pickup trucks and Scoliosis' sportscar.

Al's was a place that reminded to me very much like Paul's, the hangout in Bayporte where I had spent so many hours of my life.

Scoliosis and Ernie sat waiting for us in the rear of the restaurant. Scoliosis wore a denim jacket and his mirrored sunglasses. Ernie looked like many other coaches, just paunchier.

We sat down and nodded hidy at the two fellows.

"Are you still confused about your choices in life?" I asked Scoliosis, getting down to business.

"Bhagwan tell me to look deep inside myself for the troof," he replied.

"You can look deep inside yourself," Flash said, "while you're playing football for Northup."

"Northup is school, and school is about material suh-cess," he said. "Bhagwan say material success get in the way of spiritual growf."

Ernie said, "You're wasting your breath with this kid. Bhagwan's got him all brainwashed. All he wants is fresh water, clean air and good vibrations."

"Is that so?" I asked Scoliosis. "Is that all you really want?"

"I want what Bhagwan want me to want."

"Scoliosis," Flash said, "would you play football if Bhagwan wanted you to do that?"

"Bhagwan say football a waste of time."

"Maybe Bhagwan will change his mind," I said.

"Who can change Bhagwan's mind?" Scoliosis asked.

"Benjamin Franklin," I said.

"Don't know him."

"Bhagwan knows Benjamin. Bhagwan likes him a lot. He collects pictures of Benjamin."

Scoliosis said he would do as Bhagwan said.

"We'd like to meet Bhagwan," I told him.

Scoliosis said at that moment the holy man sitting under a tree in front of the courthouse.

Bhagwan, a black man with a beard, wore sunglasses and a white cap. He had a bedsheet draped over him and his feet were encased in white Air Jordans. We could find no other holy men nearby. He had to be Bhagwan Ram Dass.

Flash and I sat down next to him and told him who we were.

"You are men of virtue and respect. I can tell by your aura," Bhagwan said.

"Bhagwan," I said, getting down to business, "we have a man up in Canada who is full of despair."

"That is unfortunate," he said.

"Well, we believe you can help him. He wants very badly for Scoliosis to play football for Northup University. Our friend is willing to donate a great deal of money to your church, or your ministry, or whatever you call it."

"I have no church or ministry," Bhagwan told us. "I have only these simple possessions and my humble beliefs about what is right or wrong."

"Our friend believes you would find your stay on Earth a bit easier to bear if you had a million dollars in the bank," Flash said.

"Tell me more," said Bhagwan.

"Our friend," I said, "is named Larry Rawson. He lives up in Canada and he is very rich. While he is a Christian, he respects your beliefs. He believes you would be able to continue your good works in reaching out to others if you had a million dollars deposited into the First Bank of Louisiana."

Flash said, "Bhagwan, I've lived a while and done

my share of things, and I can tell you something that even a holy man like yourself would agree with: Money is a nice thing to have."

"Amen to that," said Bhagwan with a solemn nod.

I said, "Mister Rawson says he will make half his gift to you immediately and the other half when Scoliosis signs his letter of intent in February. How do you feel about this?"

Bhagwan frowned a bit. Then he put his hands together in prayer, looked up to the heavens and sat quite still for a moment or two.

Then he lowered his head, opened his mouth and said, "This gift would be in American dollars?"

We got back into the rental car and headed to the airport. I rolled up the windows, blasted the air conditioning and put on a Jeter Davis CD.

When we were a few miles out of Merde, I asked Flash, "Do you think Lord Larry ever figured out that Rickey is Bhagwan?"

Flash laughed. "I don't think Larry gives a crap so long as Scoliosis ends up in a Kodiaks jersey."

SIXTEEN

Tia, if anything, looked even more beautiful than usual as she sat across from me in Ivan's, a legendary seafood restaurant in Seattle. I wanted to introduce her to Pacific Northwest cuisine, and Ivan's seemed the obvious place for that.

"Delish!" she said, swallowing a mouthful of clam chowder. She gulped down some iced tea and said, "Do you like yours unsweetened? I do."

"I'm Canadian, and unsweetened iced tea doesn't exist up there."

"Too bad for Canada."

I smiled. "Have you done much restaurant-hopping in New York? They claim to be one of the culinary capitals of the world, but I don't think I've had a dozen good meals there. Maybe they do good soul food and kosher there, but they can't cook what I like. Perogies and sausage, liver and onions, every kind of seafood. The stuff every growing Canadian boy needs."

Tia gobbled down some more food. "This is way too yummy. Salmon, shrimp, halibut? Bill Gates should come by and eat here. He's not that far away."

"I think he eats at McDonald's," I said. "He devours his food without tasting it, then goes back to work."

"He needs to slow down, do less and smell the coffee."

"He would probably tell us to speed up, do more and never mind the fucking coffee."

Tia had flown in from New York just a few hours

earlier. She'd checked into the Emerald City Inn, a few floors below Flash and me. She said she'd slept during the flight and felt wide awake and totally disoriented.

"I guess that's part of my job." She sighed. "I get on a plane, conk out, wake up in a huge, unfamiliar city, check into a fancy hotel and get busy. Then I leave town and do the same thing all over again."

The Emerald City Inn, a dark-green, circular monument to high-tech wealth, had forty stories of spacious suites offering magnificent views of Puget Sound. The inn occupied the sites of small SROs that had sat there for decades, always full of poor people grateful for a place to sleep. I preferred the quiet elegance of the older, lovingly restored hotels to the ostentatious places like the Emerald City Inn, with its garish spirals of green neon that were visible to airborne passengers thousands of feet above the city.

Before my dinner with Tia, I called Sheri in Los Angeles and told her about my adventure in Merde, Louisiana. She covered her phone with her hand and howled with laughter at the image of Bhagwan Rickey in his Air Jordans and her father falling for Rickey and Scoliosis' nonsense.

"Remember," I said, "that's a million less you'll be getting some day in his will."

"Doesn't matter. Sounds to me like Bhagwan and Scoliosis need it more than I do."

Lord Larry had a billion-dollar international business empire, so I could understand how easily his daughter could shrug off his big payout to those shyster brothers.

Sheri told me she had the weekend free and wanted to fly up to Seattle.

I said no. It would be a boring football game and dinner with the guys.

"Everyone getting along OK?" she asked.

"Everything's fine," I said.

"Miss me?"

"Always."

"I should fly up, then," she said.

"I'll fly down when I can."

I had invited Flash to have dinner with Tia and me at Ivan's, but he had declined. He wanted to cruise the bars surrounding U. Dub and screw whichever drunken, vulnerable coeds had been dumped by their boyfriends that week.

Tia, sick of iced tea, ordered a locally brewed beer. "I've been thinking of going veggie," she said. "Even vegan."

"Why?"

"Well, do you know how abominably we treat the animals we raise for food?"

"I think they were put here for us to eat," I said. "We have to raise billions of animals to feed us all, so we probably mistreat them before we kill them and eat them."

"And all that meat we're consuming? Is it really good for our bodies. I think some people have a giant slab of meat for breakfast, lunch and dinner." She shuddered. "All that cholesterol! I really think people get cancer from such a high meat intake."

"I guess you're right." I drank down my double Canadian Comfort over ice and said, "But I could never go veggie nor vegan. Pork chops taste good. Chicken tastes good. Steak tastes good."

"Sewer rat might taste like pumpkin pie for all I know, but I'd never put the filthy thing in my mouth."

"If you went vegan, you wouldn't be able to go to the movies and eat buttered popcorn. You know what bugs me? They don't even have buttered popcorn at movie theaters any longer. They top the popcorn with butter-flavored vegetable oil. Isn't that disgusting?"

"Doesn't matter to me," she said. "I don't eat junk food."

Soon we went back to the Emerald City Inn and I insisted we go into the bar for a nightcap.

We sat at the bar, on stools, rather than at one of the booths or one of the sofas. The bar seemed deserted, which, to me, was the best kind. The Emerald City Inn had a reputation for being home to the fanciest bar in town. If this one sat virtually empty, I wondered how unoccupied all the other bars in downtown Seattle were on that evening, and how they all managed to survive.

We sat together, our knees almost touching. She ordered a Canadian Comfort over ice, just like me.

"Back at the restaurant," I told her, "you stayed sober but I got pissed. So, now that I'm here and you're here and I'm drunk, I should tell you that if you try to take advantage of me tonight, I won't exactly fight you off and I think I would even respect you in the morning."

"Poor baby," she said—and then she leaned over and kissed me hard. I gestured to the bartender for the check.

"Shall we go upstairs," I said, "so that you can take advantage of me?"

"Red," she whispered, "I'm not going to bed with you tonight. Not that I don't want to, but...no, it's not going to happen."

"Let's go on upstairs anyway. We can talk about it some more."

She shook her head. "I like to think of you as a friend, and sex would cheapen that. I want to have Sheri as a friend, too. I admire you both so much."

I sighed. "You *know* it's going to happen sooner or later, don't you?"

She frowned and sat back a bit. "No, I don't know that at all. It won't happen if I say no." Then, "Another thing I wanted to tell you about. When we first met, I could tell right away that you were attracted to me, and I liked that a lot. Imagine! Red Crossley, football hero, is interested in me, Miz Nobody."

"I'm talking about a one-nighter, not a long-term commitment."

"Well," she said, "I'm deeply in love with someone and want you two to meet so we can all be friends."

"Tomorrow morning, I'll call your boyfriend personally and tell him how lucky he is."

Tia laughed and scribbled her name on the check. In the elevator, she yawned and looked out at the city below. I concluded that she would not be sexually exploiting me that night.

I walked her to her door. She gave me the briefest and most sisterly of hugs and a peck on the cheek.

"I value you, Red. I think the world of you," she said. "See you in the morning, OK?"

"Tonight has been educational for me," I said.

"You mean that now you know I'm attached?"

I laughed. "No, not that. no girl who looks like you could ever be single for more than fifteen minutes. No, tonight I learned that my wife knows me better than I know myself."

Feeling an extraordinary sense of gratitude to Tia for not letting me screw her while my wife was a thousand miles away, I moseyed on over to the elevator and pressed the up button. When the car arrived, I turned around and waved goodnight at Tia, and she waved back before shutting her door.

In my suite, I turned on my TV and watched some insipid movie I had already seen on one of my many long flights.

At about ten o'clock on Saturday morning, we prepared for the Flash Gortton in our suite. We had two cameras, lapel microphones, lights and Tia as our boss.

Tia had to shush Stevie to stay quiet and tell her not to move around while the cameras rolled.

Stevie Parkerson, a U. Dub coed, had spent the night with Flash. A lithe, doe-eyed cutie who looked a year or two under the legal drinking age, Stevie had on one of Flash's shirts and not much else. She scowled when Tia told her to turn off the TV so that they could begin the interview, so Stevie curled up on a sofa and lit up one of Flash's bombers. "OK if I smoke?" she asked, rolling her eyes.

"Yes," said Tia. "Have a beer, too. There're some in the minibar."

"Rad!" Stevie jumped up, popped open a can of Budweiser, and spread out on the sofa as she drank, smoked and watched the interview.

Within minutes, she got a bit restless and started rearranging herself on the sofa. Some of Flash's shirt rode up on her. We could see Stevie's thighs as she crossed and uncrossed her legs. Then we saw some bare snatch, which bothered her not at all but compromised the cameraman's ability to concentrate.

"Want to go to the game?" he asked Stevie. "I have a ticket for you."

"I don't like the Seahawks," she told him. "I've never forgiven them for losing that Super Bowl against the Steelers." She sucked hard on the joint and held down the smoke. "You just do your interview thing and I'll shut up."

Tia, for the past several minutes, had kept staring at Stevie. I couldn't tell if her eyeballing was because of Stevie's beauty and nakedness, or Tia's disgust and fascination over this airheaded little slut Flash had picked up and screwed.

"Action!" Tia said.

I introduced myself and Flash. I reminded everyone that he and I had known each other forever and that he had gotten all the top NFL honors. Now he was a writer, a controversial one. I managed to keep the smirk off my face as I spoke to my oldest and best friend—how could we sit there and do this interview without pretending we were a couple of kids goofing around? But Flash, a far better actor than I, nodded and spoke with an admirable seriousness.

"I had to write that article, Red. I knew bad things were happening in the NFL and it was keeping me awake at night."

"Ted Charles was a bad offender," I said.

"He was the worst but not the only one. He's probably got Swiss bank accounts where he's stashed the money he's won from fixing games."

"You wrote that Charles allegedly manipulated the scores of games."

"Oh, there's nothing 'alleged'; I *know* he did it."

"The person who told you so is a nude dancer."

"I have other sources. I just won't name them."

"What about the other NFL officials? Any bad ones?"

"I can't prove it, but my opinion is that the corruption is widespread. So many games have looked like they've come out of Ripley's Believe It or Not."

"Aren't you taking the word of some pretty shady characters?"

"Maybe," Flash said. "But so what?"

"You've written that the players are deliberately giving NFL fans a mediocre brand of football and will persist in doing so until the owners wake up to what's happening and meet the players at the bargaining table."

"Yessir. The players have the power to turn every game into a great big joke, and if you ask me, they've been doing just that. If the owners aren't worried, they should be."

"I'm not sure that destroying the sport would benefit anyone," I said.

"The sport would survive. The NFL would die. Someone else would come along and start a new league. The players would go back to work."

"Countless fans out there feel differently. They're excited about the NFL and want it to continue indefinitely."

"Too bad for them if they like the inferior product they've been getting. Vast numbers of people pay good money to watch Hollywood crap, too. Give people Big Macs all their lives and they probably won't even know that filet mignon exists."

Flash decided not to attend the Seahawks-Invaders

game on Sunday. Too many people would want to ask him about his *Playboy* article—or punch him in the nose.

He stayed in with Stevie, a girl he liked and somehow admired. He thought she might be the one he had sought all his life. She was certainly pretty—he felt offended by female ugliness and considered his repulsion natural and normal. Also, she felt utterly unashamed that her only ambitions in life were eating, sleeping, screwing and getting high.

Flash had asked her to fly to New York and move in with him. She could be his muse and escort while he worked on his novel. Her life with him in Manhattan would be consist of what she had been doing with him that weekend in Seattle.

Her indefinite absence from U. Dub would be easy to deal with, she said. She could do her work online or not at all.

"You know what I love most about Stevie?" Flash asked me. "She just lives for the moment, man. She just keeps everything nice and simple."

Tia had never been to King County Stadium, so I took her for a tour. We started in the Seahawks Club, a big, private place for dining, drinking, dancing and seducing, or even watching the game if one were still sober enough to do so. To me, the Seahawks Club was not unlike Pandora's Box back in Bayporte.

Next, Tia and I sneaked around the stadium's private suites, whose doors were wide open due to the early hour. We peeked inside some of them and waved at the partygoers, a few of whom actually waved back.

"Each suite is decorated differently," Tia said, with the wide-eyed wonder of a child being taken through the White House.

"Yeah," I said, "they buy the suites and fix them up the way they like.

We saw a French Provincial living room, an Art Deco patio, an Early American library, a harem, an aquarium, a gymnasium, an aviary and a bare room in which half a dozen flight attendants stood about sipping wine.

"Let's go bum a drink off Jack," I said to Tia as I led her to the visiting owner's suite. I no longer had any ambivalence about hanging out with Tia or introducing her to Jack and Kathleen or any other people Sheri and I knew. Tia was simply my personal assistant and stage manager.

Jack shook Tia's hand and practically drooled.

"Look at this poor girl's face and body," he said as he checked her out. "She's just tragic. Red, how can you stand to be around this poor creature."

"I'm a professional, Jack. I work with whoever they give me."

"Nice to meet you, too, Jack," Tia said with a giggle.

"Did you say you were Red's 'personal assistant'?" Kathleen asked her, shooting me a look that said, *Has Sheri met this gorgeous young thing yet? Is she OK with it?*

"I'm the broadcast team's *stage* manager," Tia said.

"Hmm," Kathleen said.

Con Horwitz welcomed our TV audience to "a wild

one in the great Pacific Northwest, where birds caw and sharks patrol the chilly waters of Seattle."

Con nodded to me for a comment before the game started.

"I don't know how many sharks are hanging out this far north," I told him, "but I'm pretty sure Nordstrom could order one in for you."

The Seahawks scored three unanswered touchdowns in the first quarter and from then on just played conservative football, killing time as the Invaders' quarterback, Vernon Braithwaite, who, with no Red Crossley or Flash Gortton to save his ass, threw away the ball or ran out of bounds.

"What a job the Seahawks have done today by paralyzing the Invaders with their 'All on One' defense!" Con shouted, not knowing that Seattle had abandoned their 'All on One' years earlier.

Towards the end of the first half, we watched as the network cut away to a recent game in San Diego. Ted Charles appeared on the screen, refereeing a Chargers game. The crowd there at Jack Murphy Stadium cheered for him, and he doffed his cap.

Con, who apparently didn't read *Playboy* or pay much attention to the world around him, said when the network threw it back to us, "What a fine tribute to the guys on the field who keep the action from getting out of hand. I don't know how much the NFL pays those guys, but if you ask me, they deserve a raise!"

I stood straight up and looked down at the football field early in the third quarter. I heard Tia's excited voice on my headset.

"Oh my God! Sheri Rawson—you're here!"

Your old lady's come by to check up on you, asshole, my

little inner voice told me.

I turned around, saw Sheri in the broadcast booth, and went over to give her a kiss.

"Glad you could make it," I told her.

"Are you?" Her eyes darted in Tia's direction.

Marrying into spectacular wealth is not always the best thing a man can do. Her family probably owns a Gulfstream jet, and if it happens to be parked at LAX, and his wife is there, too, she can board that Gulfstream and say, "Take me to Seattle so I can surprise my hubby," and the pilot will fly her to Sea-Tac International Airport. Once there, she can get a taxi and be at King County Stadium, where she can surprise her man, get the impression that he's *shtupping* his stage manager, divorce him and make him unhappy forever.

Without that money, there is no Gulfstream. She stays put, doesn't meet Tia Gomez and assumes her husband is a stand-up guy. Money is not always a nice thing to have.

In the broadcast booth, Sheri said, "Hi, Tino. Red has told me what a nice guy you are."

Tia frowned.

I said, "Sheri, this is Tia. She's our stage manager. She helps me and Con."

"Now I know why you fly out to each game a couple of days before you need to be there," my wife said through clenched teeth. "Goodbye forever, superstar!"

I followed her out of the broadcast booth. As she stood waiting for the press elevator to open, I said, "Come on, Sheri! You have the wrong idea about this! I'm no Tiger Woods! She just helps me! I'm at work!"

"Yeah, sure. Good luck with her."

SEVENTEEN

Being knocked on my ass by Painless O'Neal had been a picnic compared to my marital crisis. My father had cracked and taken off because he didn't know how else to cope with his desperately unhappy marriage.

A marital crisis, however, didn't impair my ability to function as a broadcaster. I received an Emmy nomination for spending all those hours in all those booths, making concise observations whenever Con Horwitz came up for air.

The nomination would have meant far more to me, of course, if there hadn't been quite so many categories and so many on-air people nominated. When I received news of my nomination, I figured out that all the networks had nominated their own people; ESPN had also nominated the spectacularly incompetent Con Horwitz, which, to me, cheapened my nomination significantly.

I deserved an Emmy, or something, only if they were comparing me to Con. But I still wanted to win the award, if only to convince myself that I was still worthy of something despite my breakup with Sheri.

No one in our world—especially me—could believe that we had separated, and our friends were powerless to intervene. Naturally, many of them reached out to her to take me back—Flash, L.T., Jack Piros, Painless, even Tia, who surely had nothing to say that my wife wished to hear. Flash, the brother Sheri and I'd never had, had even flown out to California to talk her into reconciling with me. She gave him a welt under his eye.

I had spoken to her myself, but pride, like an angry, strong man, had clamped its hand over my mouth and prevented me from saying what I knew she needed to hear.

The day after Sheri's appearance in the broadcast booth I Seattle, I had gone back to Westwood House and we'd had a long verbal tussle that left us breathless and soul-sick.

"Sheri," I had said, "this is our first real spat. It could be the chance for us to show each other what kind of people we really are."

"Oh, you've already shown me your true colors."

"You have it all wrong about Tia Gomez and me. She means nothing to me. I don't know why I lied to you about her. I was a fool to do that. It's just that pretty women don't like to hear that their husbands are working with other good-looking women. Right?"

"Tia Gomez isn't just good-looking," my wife told me, "she's a heartbreaking, homewrecking Latin goddess."

"She's just a kid out of college. She wants to get ahead. She's seen me on TV lots of times, so she thinks I'm famous. She hasn't been around long enough to know any better."

"So she flashes her vag at you, but you say, 'No thanks, I'm married'? Am I supposed to believe that?"

"Hello?" I said, my voice unwisely laden with sarcasm. "Which part of 'nothing happened' didn't you understand?"

"Oh, I understood what you did. I just didn't believe a fuckin' word of it."

"Nothing happened."

"You're a lyin' sack of shit," she said.

"No—"

"You're a lyin' son of a bitch."

"Wrong, wrong, wrong. Why are you so totally convinced that shit happened?"

Sheri snarled. "Because I've met *her* and I'm *married* to *you*. You're your Uncle Rex's nephew, a pussy hound. How could you *do* that?"

I snarled back. "What *exactly* have I done?"

"You cheated on me and lied about it. How many Tias have there been that I don't know about? You seem to forget that I've known you all my life. When it comes to women, you are addicted. Women and Canadian Comfort are the two great vices in your life. You don't have any 'just say no' inside of you."

"Then why did you marry me?"

"Because I thought you had outgrown that kind of behavior."

"Sorry to disappoint you," I said.

"Not half as sorry as I am," she retorted.

I sighed. "You're just angry, Sheri. You're angry over something that didn't happen. I did give you the wrong idea, and I apologize for that. But you don't stop loving someone over these minor transgressions."

I stepped towards her, but she froze me with a look that said, *Come closer and I'll kick your balls up through the roof of your mouth.*

"Sheri, I think you would like Tia."

"I seriously doubt that."

That was a dumbass thing to say, my little inner guiding voice told me.

"Tia respects you, Sheri." I winced at the words.

"Why? Because she's banging my husband and I don't seem to mind?"

"Speaking of people we respect, you certainly seem

to have a high opinion of Sully Jackman."

"What's that supposed to mean?"

"Maybe you're doing with him what you accuse me of doing with Tia."

"Uh, I don't think so, and I resent you for saying such a thing. This hotel room is mine. I want you to leave."

"We're married, Sheri. We have work to do. We need to straighten things out."

"Hey, did someone just turn on the radio to the Doctor Joy fucking Browne show?" She marched over to the door and opened it. "Shoo."

"Just walk out? Is that what you want?"

She nodded. "You're not quite as dumb as you seem, Bubba."

"And do what? Where do you expect me to go?"

"Call Tia and ask her to put you up for a few nights. If she says no, call Flash. If he says no, hop a flight back to Bayporte. You still have a home there, right?"

"If I leave, you may never see me again."

"Is that a threat or a promise?"

"Sheri, you really have no right to treat me this way."

"Don't I? We've been married for five years and I'm starting to wonder how many other Tias you've fucked."

"Zero, including Tia," I said.

Had I gone to bed with Tia? No. Had it occurred to me to do so? Hell yes.

EIGHTEEN

I dislike the Super Bowl, regardless of where it is played or by whom. I suppose it could be fun if one had just been released after being locked up somewhere for a long time. The NFL likes to think of Super Bowl Week as an event of profound cultural significance, but those who have actually been to the host city during that time knows it is merely a week-long drunk followed by a lopsided game likely decided by the second quarter. Some years ago, the San Francisco 49ers met the San Diego Chargers and trounced them, 49-26. Most of the hung over fans in humid Miami that year, witnessing the expected blowout, seemed surprised that the Chargers kept things as close as they did.

I felt this way even as a Bayporte Invader, when, much more recently, I stumbled with my boys into the big game which, by the luck of the lottery, ended up being played in our very own downtown stadium, Great Elizabeth Place. I remember feeling, first as a player and then as a broadcaster, that the Super Bowl appeared to be for something besides letting two teams have at it for four quarters to see who gets the bragging rights as the world champions. *My* impression was that the Super Bowl existed for everyone to worship the National Football League, celebrate the commissioner's good health and feel smug about the million-dollar TV spots the network had sold.

This year, the big game was in Oakland, and I liked that. I had always been fond of the Bay Area. ESPN had virtually taken over the entire Jack London Hotel, a big, hip waterfront establishment named for the tragic, legendary writer who penned many of his best stories in that city.

Neither the 49ers nor Raiders had made it into the postseason, but the people of Oakland seemed to think that hosting the Super Bowl was a good reason to get drunk and obnoxious in the street. We in the Jack London had our own swimming pool, bars and restaurants, so we were protected from the chaos, except that the network had invited a few thousand people who might want to bug Red Crossley for a cell-phone picture, so there was that.

I had secured two extra rooms for Flash and Phil Ruble and their guests. Flash had brought Stevie and Phil was there with Betty Jean. Stupid men, I thought. Two minutes in the Jack London taught me that the joint had Stevies and Betty Jeans of all colors and bra sizes.

Flash had flown out to Oakland against his better judgment. "I try to avoid tens of thousands of drunks if I can," he said.

Fortunately, his suite, courtesy of ESPN, had a balcony, which meant he could look down upon the masses but they had no access to him.

Those days were filled with armies of reporters ganging up on this Seahawks punter or that Bills cornerback and pelting him with questions about how often he masturbated as a teenager.

Tia Gomez kept busy by arranging for me to do inserts on virtually all of the players on both teams, none of whom had anything to say beyond the usual "They're a tough team and we'll just have to play better than they do."

Each night, we partied. Tia and I went with Flash

and Stevie and Phil and Betty Jean on a ferry that cruised about San Francisco Bay for most of the night. The others on the boat were ad-agency people, minor movie stars and ESPN executives. We had fun anyway.

Phil Ruble looked around on that first night and said, "I have a new motto to live by: 'I love my job—it sure beats working.'"

Some of the owners confronted Flash at the parties, wanting to know if he really believed that players were dogging it, as he had written in his *Playboy* article.

"You mean you guys buy *Playboy* and read the articles?" he retorted.

Consuela Evans, the widow from Miami and Cuba who owned the Dolphins, urged Flash to return to Canada.

"You should be ashamed. Football is America's sport. If you don't like it, move back north and spend the rest of your life fishing for salmon," said Consuela. An emaciated woman in her fifties, she looked as frail and delicate as a statue made of ashes.

"You talk too much," Flash said to Consuela. "Shut up and eat a bit of something before the wind blows you away."

Jack Piros attended all the parties. Usually he drifted into the crowd, trying to elude his wife.

Back at our hotel, Tia and I sat on the balcony while the others retired to their rooms. On this evening, she told me more about her love life.

"I wouldn't consider talking about it while those other people were around. I just need to say these things to someone who will listen with empathy and tolerance. My relationship is getting complicated and could have a big impact on the rest of my life.

"It started a few years ago, when I first moved to Manhattan. I met an older man and let myself get involved with him. He pursued me and I liked that. I liked older men. Younger men bored me. Do you understand what I mean?"

I nodded.

"Good. Well, this man was in his early fifties, rich and married. Most of the women I knew at ESPN had older, married 'boyfriends.' So I thought, 'Why not?' By the way, I won't tell you his name. He's a prominent New York lawyer, but I'm sure you wouldn't recognize his name.

"Around this time, I met, purely by accident, his daughter, Valerie. We became friends. She wasn't a beauty—she wasn't even particularly pretty—but she had a deep mind and a beautiful soul.

"Valerie's father has no idea that I'm friends with her, and it needs to stay that way." She shook her head. "The hassles it would cause! Whoa!"

"Tia," I said, "I can see that he wouldn't want his daughter to know that you were his girlfriend. But if he loves you that much, he'll get a divorce."

"That's what he says he wants to do. But I don't want him to do that. It would be dreadful."

"Not dreadful at all," I said. "The divorce would be ideal. He loves you, you love him, you two get married and you resume your friendship with Valerie. Everything is copacetic."

"Red," Tia said, "I'm not in love with *him*. I'm in love with Valerie."

"Hey?" I swallowed hard and wanted her to say it again. Or maybe I wanted her to say something different because I couldn't cope with that I'd just heard.

"I said—"

I held up my hand. "It's Valerie." I wanted to scream and shout, throw a temper tantrum and wake up everyone in the hotel. But I didn't.

"She and I have something together," Tia said, her voice cool and soft. "It's so natural and perfect."

I nodded, knowing right then that I would save myself a great deal of humiliation by keeping this conversation a secret forever. Of course, I knew I would tell Flash about it one day years afterwards, when Tia had become a faded memory and my best friend and I could laugh our asses off about the time I had nearly thrown away my entire life over a dyke.

I slept poorly that night, as I always had when obsessing over a loss of some size. Tia, of course, would continue to be my stage manager and general helpmate, but I couldn't stop thinking about her Mediterranean beauty and the wonderful items she kept in her brassiere and underpants.

Valerie, I kept telling myself, was one lucky bitch.

Isaac Christopherson, the Bay Area music legend, sang the national anthem in the Oakland Coliseum. The NFL, insisting that "The Star Spangled Banner" be performed by a famous local act, wanted the Grateful Dead, but the Haight-Ashbury band refused to perform without the late Jerry Garcia; then the league wanted Journey to perform, but only if Steve Perry would sing instead of that little Filipino guy they had gotten to replace him. So that left Isaac.

The singer, and the game, bored me. What interested me was the fact that the festivities would air at six in the evening, so that ESPN and the NFL could fully exploit the primetime TV audience. It also meant that viewers would have to choose between the Super Bowl and the premiere of *Lally's Place*. Watch one while recording the other.

The game, to the surprise of very few, became so tedious that, by the time Lally's opening credits rolled, its viewership increased dramatically as Seattle overwhelmed Buffalo, 49-3. Nobody watched the game or listened to Con Horwitz and me except people too lazy or sick to reach of their TV clickers.

In the first half, Buffalo's quarterback, Monty Joel, threw a screen pass to his superstar wide receiver, Royce Jeremiah, at midfield. Jeremiah, as he so often had, appeared to be on his way to six points. But then, perhaps out of simple anxiety, he switched the ball from his right hand to his left, and scampered down the field with an infirm purchase on the pigskin. The ball struck his wildly pumping left knee and tumbled onto the natural surface. Jeremiah kicked his fumble towards the end zone and very nearly managed to smother it on the one yard line, but the ball popped out from under him like a deformed coconut and a Seahawks defender grabbed it in the end zone. Touchback.

As we ran the replay, I said, "Royce Jeremiah will do that one percent of the time, and I guess we've just seen that one percent. I'm surprised that he did it on a natural surface—that's an artificial-surface kind of fumble."

So much of the first was Monty Joel taking the snap, receiving little if any pass protection, scrambling about and throwing the ball out of bounds just as three or four Seahawks were about to dive-bomb him.

Or, Monty wouldn't be quite so fortunate and end up being knocked on his ass. His star running back, Craig Rogers, rushed for one or two yards each carry before being taken down. Monty, so anxious about the Seahawks' eagerness to break him in half, sometimes threw the pass before his receiver had even turned around to face him.

Joel, running like hell to elude speedy, ferocious defensive lineman Tad Lawrence, lofted the ball into the air and it came down as a trio of Seahawks, with no Bills in sight, took turns calling for it. One caught it and allowed his two teammates to block for him as he ran it back for a touchdown.

By halftime, this Super Bowl had become such a yawner that Colton Williams said to me through my headset, "Red, maybe you should try to liven things up a bit by saying some clever Canadian things so that people don't change the channel."

I responded by saying into my live mike, "If I were at home on a sofa with a beer, you know what I would watch? I'd check out *Lally's Place* on ABC, a sitcom that's premiering at this very moment."

Ray Michaels chimed in: "Red, you know you can't promote the competition. Better take that back."

"How come?" asked Colton Williams.

"I just told you why," Ray said. "You can't be on ESPN saying, 'This is shit. Watch ABC.'"

"So what, Ray? Let Red do his thing," Colton said.

"Yeah, Colt, and then Mark Richardson calls me and says, 'Why did you let Red tell our viewers to watch something else?'"

"Ray, nobody is watching this blowout, anyway.

Let Red have his fun telling everyone to watch *Lally's Place*. His wife's the star, you know."

I heard some sort of clicking noise in my headset.

"Ray just hung up his headset," Colton said. "It's his way of saying, 'Fuck you very much.'"

"Con," I said on the air to Horwitz, "this is becoming one of the biggest blowouts in Super Bowl history."

"It certainly is. Seattle has totally dominated this contest," he replied.

"I have an idea. Let's change the channel and watch *Lally's Place*. See if we can get it on the monitor."

Just then the phone rang in our booth. Tia answered it and handed the receiver to me.

"Mark," she said.

The boss? I mouthed.

She nodded.

Mark was back at the Jack London Hotel, watching the game with advertisers who cared only about their commercials.

"Sounds great, Red!" he said. "Do that some more!"

"Hey?"

"That *Lally* stuff. Telling people to watch it."

"Oh, that. The game is boring. I was just kidding around."

"Well, our clients have bought time on *Lally*, too. They love it that you're plugging it on ESPN."

"Ray Michaels got mad at me over it," I said.

"Ray works for me. His opinion doesn't mean shit," said Mark. "We're watching *Lally's Place* on another TV."

"Any good?"

"It has its moments. It's really Sheri's show. She's so sassy as Lally, and so gorgeous."

"So you think it has a chance-chance," I asked him, "or just a chance?"

He laughed. "I'm sure it will be a big hit."

Colton Williams told Con Horwitz to let me back on the air.

"So, Red," Con said, "didn't you predict that the Buffalo Bills would win tonight's contest over the Seattle Seahawks?"

"I don't remember, Con. But I have an update on the premiere of *Lally's Place* on ABC. Lally, played by Sheri Rawson, is reminding everyone who's boss, and Lord help those who forget it."

"The fans in the Pacific Northwest will rejoice over their team's first-ever Super Bowl victory…"

"Congratulations to the Seattle Seahawks, and congratulations, too, to ABC for being courageous enough to premiere *Lally's Place* right up against the Super Bowl. Hey, Sheri! If you're listening, break a leg on this one!"

Con did the rest of the talking. I got another call on the booth phone.

"Turned out nice, huh?"

"Yes, Painless. It was terrific."

"The Bills gave us their full cooperation. When Royce Jeremiah fumbled and kicked the ball? Greatest acting job ever. Monty Joel with his interceptions and incompletions? Bad night for Super Bowl, great night for our union."

"Players helped their own cause tonight," I said.

"How many fans left the Coliseum tonight before the fourth quarter?"

"Most of them."

Painless whooped. "Red, I'm gonna tell you a secret. I'm calling from D.C., right? Commissioner Roder had a meeting with the owners, and they're ready to give us what we want. We beat the owners just like the Seahawks beat the Bills."

"Sweet," I said.

"You deserve credit for believing in us."

"I wonder what kind of mischief you'll be up to next year."

"Me, too, Red."

We both laughed, and I handed the phone back to Tia. She put some promo cards in front of Con and he read them.

"We're a done deal," said Colton Williams from the truck. "Good work, everyone."

...

I didn't understand TV ratings very well, but those who did assured me that *Lally's Place* was a big hit. By the time the ratings were published, I had returned to Bayporte and spent much of my time missing my wife, staring at her ugly abstract paintings and wondering about my own professional future. Mark Richardson had said something about wanting me to do some other sports work for ESPN, and I didn't know what he had in mind, but the only other gigs I could get were speaking engagements on the banquet circuit. So, if ESPN wanted me to be its roving sports guy, I'd do it, as long as they paid for my airline tickets, hotel rooms and bar bills.

While I was hanging out in our condo waiting for Mark to call, I dialed Sheri down in Los Angeles.

"Sounds like you've got a hit," I said.

"I guess," she said, her voice as frigid as the dark side of the moon.

"How's it goin', sweetums?" I asked.

"OK."

"That's nice. I'm back at *our* home in Bayporte, you know. I've just been admiring your lovely Pollock paintings."

"Oh."

"I told the Super Bowl audience to turn off the game and tune into your show. Pretty smart, hey?"

"I didn't know that."

"Our condo looks as nice as ever. We have a maid come in once a week."

"Is the maid's name Tino?" she asked.

"Very funny. Aren't you ever going to put this behind you?"

"I have to go now. Very busy with work."

"OK, Sheri. I love you."

"Bye."

Click.

A day or so later, Mark Richardson called to tell me that he had decided to use me as a regular sports broadcaster, though he was still trying to decide on the specifics.

He offered me three hundred thousand dollars per year. I said yes.

"Red, I wish you had an agent. That's the way we usually do things."

"I've gotten by without one so far," I said.

"I want to send you out to golf tournaments," he said.

"Mark, I don't know a thing about that."

"Doesn't matter. Nobody watches it anyway. Just be your usual charming self and you'll be fine." Then, "Red, you're now a professional broadcaster. What do you think about that?"

"I'm still trying to sort things out," I said.

"By the way, I'll need you to attend the Emmy Awards dinner in March. It's a great way for me to show off the people I've got."

"OK." I wanted to have an excuse to see Sheri, if she was still mad at me in March. As I sat on the sofa and spoke to Mark, I looked again at Sheri's art on our walls and thought, for a sickening instant, that she might really never live here again with me.

I supposed she had a few things to feel happy about. Her show was up for several Emmys, and she might win one herself, though I really doubted that she gave a shit about that. She *really* wanted to be as funny as possible and to have as big an audience as it could get.

I had always thought that they gave out far too many Emmys and Grammys—they gave them to too many people and far too often.

"Will we win anything?" I asked Mark.

"Winning doesn't matter," he said. "It's the nomination that counts."

Flash Gortton turned off his MacBook Pro and told Stevie Parkerson to keep her hands off it, but he urged her to take a walk through Central Park each afternoon to blow the cobwebs out of her head.

He flew out to Bayporte to watch Scoliosis sign his letter of intent. It would make the young man the property of L.T. and the Kodiaks for the next four years.

Flash moved back into his old room in our

condominium, and for a little while I felt as if we were brothers and roommates again.

That evening, we all ate at Paul's Submarine Sandwich Stop—L.T., his wife Darla, Flash and me. L.T. kept smiling and laughing, his face red and merry.

"It's all done," he said. "Scoliosis signed the letter earlier today. He's ours."

"Then what's tomorrow?" I asked.

L.T. shrugged. "Just a bunch of bullshit for the media. The signed letter is already in the lawyer's vault. We get the boy to sign another one tomorrow while they take his picture."

The coach also told us about the alumni award that was supposed to be a big secret. The U. had decided to start a tradition—the Big Bear Award—a plaque presented to the Northup graduates who had gone out into the world and done some big things.

"You and Sheri are the co-winners. They might have included Flash, but he wrote that story for the beaver magazine and got some people pretty mad," L.T. told us.

"They call it the Big Bear, eh?" I said.

"Yes, because a Kodiak's a bear, right? You and your missus will be our first two Big Bears."

"Do we have to?"

"The ceremony won't be until next September. They'll present the plaques to you at halftime."

"Maybe by then Sheri will love me again," I muttered.

"Sorry you won't be a Big Bear, Flash," L.T. said, "but you know how it is."

"I still have my writing and my muse," he said.

"How's your muse, anyway?" L.T. asked.

"She's the same—eating, sleeping, doping, screwing."

Darla frowned. "What *are* you guys talking about?"

"Flash is writing another novel," I said. "Nobody liked *Action Man*, but fuck them. He's sharing his Manhattan condo with a U. Dub dropout who inspires his creativity."

"What's your novel about?" Darla asked.

"It's about life," Flash said.

"Whose? Yours? Mine? Ours?" she asked.

Flash smiled. "Yes, exactly."

"I like Scott Turow's novels," Darla said.

"Well," Flash told her, "my novel is what Turow might have written if he had gone to Oliver Johnson High."

I drank down another Diefenbaker beer and said, "I want to ask each of you how to get Sheri Rawson to love me again."

"Quit porking Tia Gomez," Flash said.

"I haven't porked her, dumbass."

"Too bad for you," he retorted.

"Red," Darla said, "you should fly down there right away and beg her to take you back."

I shook my head. "She has no use for beggars."

"Oh, I'm sure she would take you back if she knew you were remorseful and sincere."

"Not till he quits porking that spick," Flash said.

"Fuck you, Flash," I said.

"You don't want to fuck *me*, Red, any more than I want to fuck *you*. You want to fuck Sheri and Tia. I want to fuck my little muse back in New York."

Darla Briggs said, "You guys just keep talking all the trash while there's a lady present. I won't be offended."

...

Scoliosis Robinson signed his letter of intent in Northup University's Alumni Lounge at noon. Phil Ruble attended the ceremony, as did two dozen other media people who formed a semicircle in front of L.T., Lord Larry, Flash and me.

Lord Larry introduced the school's two new recruits as their cue to enter the room. Rickey Robinson came in with Scoliosis and DeShonn as flashbulbs and eyes popped. Camera operators whirled about to get the best images of the two football studs.

Rickey Robinson looked exhilarated and affluent in his new Brooks Brothers suit, as did DeShonn Jones in *his* new suit.

Scoliosis wore his usual warmup suit and sunglasses, and his smile was even cockier. I admired his beautiful white teeth and wondered how many of our sorority sisters he would pork once he got settled in here.

L.T., standing and applauding, introduced Rickey.

"This is a wonduhful day for No'thup University," Rickey said in his deep, American-accented voice. "As everyone here is aware, DeShonn Jones and Scoliosis Robinson have announced their intention of playin' football for the No'thup Kodiaks, so today you are gettin' to meet the two best college athletes on the planet."

Lord Larry took out a gold pen and handed it to Rickey, who handed it to Scoliosis.

"Sign the form, my man," Rickey said to Scoliosis.

"Where I do it?"

"Right where it says."

I looked over, wondering if Scoliosis would write

Boobies. But no; he signed it legibly and spelled it right.

Everyone congratulated Scoliosis and DeShonn and shook each man's hand. All those who wanted to pose for cell-phone pictures with the two newest Kodiaks got their wishes.

L.T. then spoke to the media, beaming like a man, deeply in debt and pursued by gun-wielding creditors, who had just discovered he owned the sole Powerball winning ticket.

"I'm sure you know what this day means to me. I came here because Northup University wanted me to turn the Kodiaks into a winning team, and I knew I had to get some first-rate players to have a team we could be proud of. All I can say now is, Northup will be the team to beat!"

The media people wanted to know what Scoliosis would be majoring in at Northup.

"I be studyin' camoonication," he said. "You don't have nothin' if you don't have camoonication."

After everyone was all talked out and only a few people remained, Lord Larry grabbed my arm and pulled me into a corner.

"What's the deal with you and my daughter?"

"She's mad at me. She won't speak to me. I keep hoping she'll chill out so I can fly down there and we can reconcile."

His face was stern. "She says you're screwing around. *Are* you?"

"Would I tell *you*?"

He laughed despite himself. "Good answer."

"Larry," I said, "Her name is Tia. She's pretty. She goes on the road with us, so everyone's thinking, 'He must be porking her.'"

"Aren't you mad at this Tia? She's broken up your

home."

"*She* hasn't done a thing to me. Sheri moved out of our Bayporte condo and into a Los Angeles hotel room to do that TV show. It was of her own volition. I wish she would come back to me." Then, "What about that TV director? She spends plenty of time with him, you know. She stays the night with him."

"My daughter the fag hag," Lord Larry said.

"Why do you say that?"

"He's a fag. That business is full of them."

"Not all," I said. "Some are married."

Lord Larry smirked. "Rock Hudson was married."

"Have you heard anything from Bhagwan?"

Lord Larry shook his head. "Gone and forgotten. Next thing, he'll probably start writing self-help books like Flash did. What was his book called?"

"*What to Do When Life's a B*tch.*"

Lord Larry laughed. "Yeah, what a title. Have you read it?"

"I bought a copy at the airport bookstore here. They had about three million of 'em."

"Yeah, but have you *read* it?"

I smiled. "No, but I've known its author all my life, so I probably know what's in it."

"So he's gone forever now, hey? Moved out to New York to spend the rest of his life writing."

I shrugged. "So he says. He's got a pile of money in the bank. He's writing all the time and seems less weird than ever."

"He's still pretty weird." Lord Larry frowned for a moment. "

"I envy his sense of purpose right now. The sales and reviews mean little to him. He does it to do it," I said. "On the subject of having a purpose in life, remind your daughter that I love her."

Phil Ruble and I drove Flash out to the airport. On our way, we ate again at Paul's Submarine Sandwich Stop.

"Flash, stay over another night," Phil said. "Your hassles in New York will still be there when you get back. We have new titty bars here you haven't seen yet."

"Wish I could," Flash said, "but my muse keeps phoning to say that if I don't come home soon, she'll drink herself into an alcoholic coma."

NINETEEN

Sheri's wide, gleaming smile made me flash back to when we were nine years old, smug little brats who thought we owned the world, or at least our corner of it. A moment later we hung out in the wide hallways of Oliver Johnson High School. Then we took a walk under the myriad trees at Northup University. Finally, I pictured us boning like porn stars in New York, Los Angeles or Bayporte.

These images started up in my head because she and I noticed each other at the Emmys. Tia and I had entered the Grand Ballroom of the Westin Los Angeles and sought out our network friends; instead, I spotted Sheri, who sat with some of the *Lally* people—Sully, Arnold Shapiro, Faith Podborsky, a couple of heavies and Kathleen Piros.

The warmth of Sheri's smile lured me over to her table. I hustled Tia over there; Sheri stood up and wrapped her arms around me. I inhaled her scent and held that body I knew so well. I would have burst into tears if I hadn't been a professional broadcaster simply attending an industry event.

"I didn't know you owned one of these," Sheri said, tugging at the lapel of my tuxedo.

"It's rented," I said. "I try not to think about who's worn it before me and what they did while they were in it."

"You should rent one more often," she said.

"I would, but I'd get laughed at wearing a monkey suit in Paul's Submarine Sandwich Stop."

Sheri and Tia wore gowns that showed off most of their beautiful breasts. I stood between them, smiling and smug, convinced I had the admiration and envy of whichever heterosexual men were in the room.

"Hi, Tia. Nice to see you." Sheri reached over and gave Tia's hand a sisterly squeeze.

"You too, Sheri. You look magnificent. And congratulations on *Lally's Place*. It's the biggest thing on TV."

"Thanks," she said.

Tia pointed behind her and said, "Our table's over there. I better go join them." She walked over to the ESPN table where Mark Richardson sat with Mike Greenberg, Con Horwitz and a few others.

I looked around the *Lally* table and saw many pairs of eyes staring at me. I nodded and grinned hello.

"Red," Sully Jackman said, "you're doing great on the air. Don't let any of those network assholes try to change your style. You're very natural and engaging."

"Thanks. Don't worry—they couldn't change me if they tried. I'm just being Red Crossley. I don't know how to be anyone else. I couldn't learn a new persona if the slickest flack in town tried to teach me."

"So," I said to Sheri, "are you going to win anything tonight?"

"Nope. Natascha McElhone is the overwhelming favorite."

"Never heard of her," I said.

"Are you kidding? Haven't you ever watched Californication?"

"No," I said. "That's past my bedtime." Then, "You know, I'm not dating Tia. She's just my escort tonight. She's in a relationship."

Sheri nodded. "Flash says she's with the CEO of some Silicon Valley outfit."

"I would have told you but you haven't been accessible to me lately," I said.

"The thing is starting," she said. "You better go to your table."

"I want you back, Sheri. Let's have a long talk tomorrow."

She shook her head. "Can't. I'm flying out tomorrow to promote the show. I'm all booked up here and there for the next several months. I'm renting a house so I don't have to live in a hotel. *Lally's Place* is huge right now and Terrence Malick wants me in his next picture." She rolled her eyes and laughed. "Everyone wants a piece of Sheri Rawson."

"My wife, the queen of all media. Who woulda thunk? Back when we were kids in Bayporte—"

"That's all ancient history."

"Last time I checked, we were still married."

"Only on paper, Red."

I ignored that. "My career advisors want me to learn golf and enter tournaments."

"Sounds like fun."

"Does it? I know less than zero about golf."

"Your advisors can help you with that."

I let out a big sigh. "Gimme a fuckin' break."

"As they sing in those country songs, 'I'm doin' the hurt dance. I'm gonna keep doin' the dance till the hurtin' stops.'"

"Well," I said, "when and if the hurtin' stops, I'm on Facebook, Twitter, YouTube and everywhere else. You'll have an easy time finding me." I turned around and headed over to the ESPN table.

And did I ever get fucked up.

The awards bullshit lasted over three hours. They handed out the important Emmys during the middle of the broadcast because that was when most of the affluent viewers had tuned in.

I sweet-talked our server into bringing me double Canadian Comforts over ice while my tablemates drank wine and nibbled at their vegetables and rubber chicken.

Throughout the evening, I sat in a morose alcoholic stupor and watched as actors, directors, writers and producers went up and received statuettes for shows of which I was totally ignorant.

Sheri smiled and applauded as Natascha McElhone won for *Californication*. Natascha, as she passed by Sheri, bent down and gave my wife a little hug, reciprocated.

"How come she talks funny?" I whispered to Tia Gomez as Natascha McElhone held up her Emmy and thanked everyone she had ever met.

"She has a British accent," said Tia.

"Then how come she's on a show set in California? Does she play a British refugee or something?"

"She plays an American named Karen. She delivers her lines in a generic American accent."

"Couldn't they find an American to play Karen?"

"Shut up, Red."

Sheri cheered and shouted "Yea!" when Arnold Shapiro and Faith Podborsky rose to accept the Emmy for writing *Lally*, even though Sheri and Sully Jackman had salvaged the rat's nest of a pilot that Arnold and Faith had penned.

At the microphone, Faith swallowed often and spoke with a nervousness I would never have expected.

"This...belongs...to...the...whole...team," she

managed to say before letting Arnold take over.

"Working together makes good things happen," he said. "We look forward to having Lally and her friends around for a long time."

By the time the sports Emmys began, I felt tired and cranky. "I won't win," I told Tia, "but if I do, I hope I don't make a fool of myself in front of the worldwide TV audience."

"Don't sweat it," she said. "The telecast ended two hours ago. It's just us here, with out smart phones. If you goof up your speech, people will tweet about you but that's all."

The winner in my category, sports analyst, turned out, inexplicably, to be Tanner Wherry, a twenty-something beach boy who covered surfing for ABC.

I zoned out and let my mind wander a bit until I heard Con Horwitz exclaim "Wow!" as he jumped up and bounded up to the stage.

"What's happening?" I asked Tia, who sneered and looked up with narrowed eyes at Con.

"He's just won an Emmy," she said.

"I didn't know they gave one for Asshole of the Year."

"They do now," she said, laughing despite herself. Then she shuddered a bit. "This industry…"

"Is phonier than a three-dollar bill."

Con accepted his Emmy and spoke for so long that a few people worked up the nerve to leave, then others did, too, and soon Con was mostly just talking to himself about how great it felt to be Con Horwitz.

...

Throughout the spring and summer I attended so many golf tournaments that I could scarcely tell one from another. I traveled to Georgia, South Carolina,

Ohio, Illinois and Connecticut, all to watch men hit little white dimpled balls into holes.

Tia Gomez ended up working with me again. The network had given her a golf assignment, which pleased her because the action was live. Her job, so far as I could tell, was to get mad at the graphics flunky for putting wrong numbers on the screen and to tell us when commercial breaks became imminent.

Occasionally, through my headset, I would hear her count down, and she sounded as coked up as a '80s disc jockey hawking tampons on the air: "J&J spot! Twenty-five!…twenty!…"

Then I heard another voice: "Tia, if you want to keep your job, take a Valium."

Tia had become just one of the crew now. We remained friends, eating and drinking together and being lazy. She looked gorgeous, of course, but now all I saw was another bright, career-driven kid in an ESPN sweatshirt and old Levi's.

One summer evening in Pittsburgh, Tia asked me out to dinner. "So we can talk about stuff like we used to," she said.

She took me to a vegan restaurant where I picked at my food, if one could actually eat that shit, and my stomach growled. Tia told me she had ended her relationship with Valerie.

"Valerie said I wasn't gay enough. She got really angry that I was so fond of you, so she found someone else and left me.

"But she was right. I'm not gay enough. I'm not gay at all. I don't know why I hooked up with her. But right now I'm feeling really good about being a woman who likes men, and I've been *so* happy that you and I are friends." She reached over and touched my hand.

"Where are we going with this, Tia?" I asked, smiling as she let her hand linger on mine. "Are you trying to get in my pants or something?"

"I just want you to know how much you mean to me, Red."

I sighed. "Tia, I'm married. I love Sheri and I want to get back with her."

"That will happen, even if you don't think so. You two were meant to be together. You've known each other for thousands of years. All I want is your friendship."

"You already have it."

"For real?"

"Absolutely."

"Can we be nice and tight like this after your reconciliation with Sheri?"

"I can't see why not," I said.

"Can we have dinner like this?"

"Anything's possible, Tia."

"Promise me we'll always be friends like we are right now, Red."

"We'll always be friends, Tia."

She nodded. "Then I think we should do it."

"Hey?"

"We should make love tonight, Red. OK?"

Another man would have had her in bed as fast as he could pay the bill and get a taxi back to his hotel. But I wasn't that man. I sat there and drank Canadian Comfort, and made small talk with Tia and very nearly wept because I missed my wife so much.

· · ·

A month later, I had an ESPN gig in the Northeast, so I visited Flash at his Manhattan apartment to see if he wanted to stop writing for a few hours and go drinking with me.

Stevie opened the door and offered me a dopey smile. She, or the apartment, or both, reeked of cannabis. Her red Charles Manson T-shirt ended at her crotch, and I couldn't tell if she had anything on underneath.

"I'm watching cable TV," she said. "*A Serbian Film*. It's totally disgusting. Wanna check it out?

"Maybe next time. Where's our boy?"

"In his office. Work, work, work. He's so boring. Come on in."

Stevie hurried back onto the living room sofa and clutched a pillow as she watched the movie on Flash's six-foot plasma high-definition TV.

Flash had converted his guest bedroom into an office. He had plenty of books, a desk and not much else. I tapped on his door. He put his MacBook Pro on his desk and asked me in.

He passed on my invitation to carouse.

"I'm very creative and productive right now," he said. "Alcohol dulls my mind."

Flash told me he would be flying out to Bayporte to see the debuts of Scoliosis Robinson and DeShonn Jones in early September.

"L.T. says those boys seem happy enough at Northup. That's probably because they haven't had to study yet. All they have to do right now is practice, chase girls and drive around town.

"Talk to Sheri lately?" he asked.

"A few times during the summer. She's still mad as hell. She's now renting a house in Brentwood because of *Lally's Place*. She plays lots of tennis and hangs out with Sully Jackman. She's going to be on the cover of one of those trashy magazines like *People* or *Us*. Can't remember which."

"I know. She flew out here to do some promotional appearances for her show. We had dinner and some heart-to-heart talks." He paused. "She really misses you."

"And *I* miss *her*. She's still got her key to our condo in Bayporte. So do you." I laughed. "I've sort of semi-moved back into our place and I keep seeing reminders of you and Sheri. Are you going to stay in New York forever, or what? You want to sell us your share of the condo?"

Flash waved me off.

"Red, your problem is that you're still shell-shocked from everything that's happened to you in the past year or so. Your concussion and retirement. Shit, man, lately you've been on the road more than Jack Kerouac. Sheri moved down to California to do that sitcom, and now there's been that misunderstanding over Tia." He blew out a huge breath. "You've had a bunch of shit to deal with lately. You both have."

"Sometimes I wish," I told my lifelong best friend, "that all three of us would just say 'Fuck it!' and become Bayporte roommates again."

Flash grinned. "Was a fun time, eh?"

"Before I go, can I see a bit of your work-in-progress?"

He handed me his MacBook Pro, and I read a paragraph. It said:

Ron, an experienced cocksman, thought he had heard everything by then. But he had not expected to learn that Tina's lover was another woman.

"You fucker," I said as I handed him back his hardware. "How did you guess about Tia?"

"By the way she kept on about how beautiful Sheri was."

"Hope you didn't blab it to everyone."

"Not me."

"Bullshit. It's too tasty not to share."

"Honest, Red."

Although he said no, I still thought Flash had told Sheri about Tia.

I felt that way for two reasons. First, the joke on me was pretty damn funny. Since we were small, the three of us had seldom let the other two get away with things. This wasn't exactly mocking someone for drinking sparkling cider, but as far as Flash was concerned, it wasn't much different, either. To him, people dumb enough to get married deserved to have the problems Sheri and I were trying to cope with. If you had any sense at all, you simply put up your umbrella when it rained and went on with the nasty business of life.

Also, there was the obvious thing that Flash would try to use Tia as a way of sending Sheri back to me: "The poor bastard was so lonely that he got a crush on a *dyke*! Sheri, isn't that just the funniest, most pathetic thing you've ever heard?" Then, of course, like all other writers, he'd put my misadventure into his novel.

But Flash would have been a fool to think that telling Sheri about Tia's sexual orientation would have assuaged my wife's bitterness and resentment. Half the time, Flash thought he possessed far more wisdom and intelligence than he actually did, and he, a lifelong bachelor and indiscriminate cocksman, knew less than nothing about marriage.

Sheri, despite her fine manners, was a considerable egotist, and I had damaged her sense of self-worth when I started lying to her about Tia's name and gender.

Really, it did not matter whether I had porked Tia, just as it meant nothing that Sheri may have gotten it on with Sully Jackman. I wanted us both to blame all this *mishigaas* on our ridiculous lifestyle and start all over.

Sheri and I were so willful and driven and proud that we risked destroying our love, and everything wonderful that he had built together, just to prove how strong and uncompromising we were.

TWENTY

We had lucked out with a clear Bayporte night in early September; the light breeze carried a hint of fall coolness. The prematurely darkening sky seemed covered with blazing stars, as if God Himself had put them in just to make things look nice.

Northup University Stadium buzzed and roared with a standing-room-only crowd of 50,000 football fans, many of them University of Toronto followers who had traveled two thousand miles to see their Varsity Blues play the Northup Kodiaks.

Flash and I wandered about the field as both teams did their pre-game activities. We exchanged puzzled glances at the sight of Northup coaches who fairly vibrated with anxiety, while the Kodiaks stifled yawns as they stretched and ran.

"What do you think?" I asked Flash.

"I just hope our boys don't fall asleep in the huddle," he said.

Scoliosis Robinson and DeShonn Jones had some difficulty staying on their feet during jumping jacks.

I gazed up at Lord Larry's box on the fifty-yard-line, looking for some sign of Sheri. None.

She said she would fly up from Los Angeles on the family jet. Uncle Rex promised to meet her at the airport and deliver her to the stadium.

Up in their box, Lord Larry and Lady Joy were dressed in brown-and-gold Kodiaks satin warmup jackets and fitted caps. Next to them sat Rickey Robinson, Scoliosis' brother, the "special assistant" to the president of Rawson Mining and Minerals. Rickey wore no Kodiaks apparel, but his blue suit looked to be a Brioni, and his paisley tie probably cost a few hundred dollars.

The Northup cheerleaders and the band formed an alleyway through which the players ran on their way back into the dressing room for last-minute words from L.T.

Flash and I waited for them to disappear, then we followed them inside.

L.T. stood before his players, his mouth grim as they sat on benches and gabbled to each other before they finally shut up and let their coach speak.

"Gentlemen," he said, "this is our biggest challenge yet. The Blues are the Canadian champions. They eat teams like us for breakfast. They're waiting to kick our asses out there tonight. Northup don't mean diddley-do to Tranno. But you know what *I* think? *I* think we're gonna hit 'em with so much razzle-dazzle that they're just gonna be staggerin' all over the field! Now let's get out there and show Tranno that we're their daddy!"

The Kodiaks didn't whoop and holler. Instead, they resumed gabbling and joking with each other as they departed the dressing room.

As I leaned against the wall near the exit, I felt overwhelmed by brown-and-gold pride and said to DeShonn Jones:

"Take care of business, DeShonn."

"Already a done deal, baby," he said. "Only the other side don't know it yet."

To Scoliosis Robinson, I said:

"Go out there and have a good game, big man."

"That's the only kind I have," he replied. "They not gonna forget *me* for a very long time."

Flash and I returned to the field and stood behind

the Kodiaks' bench as the two teams knelt to pray. I felt sure that L.T. took that opportunity to remind his boys that God didn't like players who missed tackles or dropped passes.

As the teams walked onto the field for the opening kickoff, Flash tapped me on the shoulder and pointed at Lord Larry's box.

"See anyone familiar?" he asked.

I nodded. "Sheri and Uncle Rex."

Sheri smiled and waved in our direction. Then she smiled and waved in other directions.

"I wish she didn't look so damn happy," I said.

Toronto kicked off to Northup and the ball went into the end zone and out of bounds. The Kodiaks' offensive unit rushed out onto the field in their brown jerseys and gold pants. Scoliosis wore number 1 and DeShonn Jones had 99.

The Kodiaks huddled, clapped and lined up at the 20-yard line. On their first play, Syd Jimmley, the second-string quarterback, took the snap and handed off the football to Scoliosis, who broke half a dozen tackles and lumbered 80 yards for a Northup touchdown.

"Mother*fucker*!" Flash yelled. "Did you see how hard Scoliosis hit that poor bugger? That Toronto guy's ears are gonna ring for a year!"

I looked up at Lord Larry's box and saw him and Rickey pumping their arms and beaming at each other.

The Kodiaks made their extra point and kicked off to Toronto. The Blues' three passing plays, broken up by Northup's secondary, led to a Toronto punt that went out of bounds at the 35-yard line. On first down, Syd Jimmley threw a screen pass to DeShonn

Jones, who sprinted past any number of defenders for a Kodiaks touchdown.

I checked out Lord Larry's box just in time to see him and Rickey Robinson throw themselves into each other's arms and exchange a kiss on the cheek.

Flash and I stood there for a moment watching those two men.

"If they keep that up," Flash said, "Lady Joy is going to get jealous."

"With good reason," I said. "That Rickey's a cutie."

At halftime, the Kodiaks led by a score of 42-3. Scoliosis and DeShonn had scored most of Northup's points and rushed for hundreds of yards. After Scoliosis had tumbled into the end zone for the third time, I moseyed on over to L.T.

"You were right. Coaching makes all the difference."

L.T. turned to me, his face white and breathing shallow. His lips were curved into a queer little smile.

"I don't know how much more I can stand this, Red. Success can be pretty hard on a man's vital organs."

"Oh, I think you'll learn to cope with it. The human being is a pretty resilient animal."

Sheri and Uncle Rex came down onto the field during halftime as the Northup marching band played. The university's chancellor, and someone from the school's alumni association, met Sheri and me on the sideline to present us with awards for having gone from being humble little Northup Kodiaks to being, well, whatever we had become.

Flash had gone off to take a piss in the dressing room. I wondered why our alma mater felt I deserved a distinguished alumnus award but my best friend did not. Probably, it had something to do with the fact that Flash had moved permanently to New York to write full-time, while I remained in Bayporte.

Sheri and I exchanged a courteous little kiss.

"You've done so much for Northup," I told her. "I want you to know how much your hard work has meant to everyone."

"Thank you," she replied. "How have you been?"

"Thrilled my our team's performance thus far. Delighted to be able to show my Northup pride on this enchanted evening."

"Really…?"

"No. My life sucks balls. I'm aching all over."

Uncle Rex said, "I'm a betting man, and I would have put the odds at a zillion to one against the two of you acting like this. How long have you been separated? Months now, hey? You've been stupid and selfish. Get over it, both of you."

"I've been stupid and selfish," Sheri said. "I've been neglecting what really matters."

She looked at me and smiled the way she'd done since we were little. For the first time since Painless O'Neal slammed into me, I felt no pain. Just love, light and levity.

"May I assume," I asked her, "that we're sort of married again?"

She nodded. "Yes, you may."

I looked at Uncle Rex, who had the high color and wide smile of someone who has just bet his whole world on a sure thing.

"Does Sully think it's OK for you to be here?" I asked Sheri.

"If he doesn't, too bad."

"I've been thinking," I told her, "about where I want to live and what I want to do. I've decided I just want to be with you, wherever that is."

"I love you, too," she said, "even though sometimes I don't *like* you all that much."

Before I could gather her up in my arms and cover her with a thousand sweet kisses, we were gathered up by the chancellor and the man from the alumni association and walked to the 50-yard line, where the chancellor said some things into a microphone and so did the alumni man, and I'll be damned if Sheri or I paid the slightest bit of attention to them. They stuck plaques into our left hands and pumped our right ones. Sheri and I babbled thanks and smiled at each other.

Presently they escorted us back to the sideline and we wandered over to the north end zone. There we saw Flash, standing near the tunnel leading to the dressing room.

"So Red," Sheri was asking, "did you bump uglies with that power-fucker from the network?"

"Tia? A power-fucker?" I frowned. "Well, I guess you could say she was that. And, yeah, we kinda bumped uglies."

"Surprise!" She laughed in that way she'd always had, loud and guttural and full of mischief. "Was she any good? Did she come on your cock?"

To change the subject, I said, "Have you read *What to Do When Life's a B*tch*? I don't like it."

"Flash told me about you and Tia, but that's not why I've come back to you."

"Tia who? I don't care about *why* you're back, just that you are."

I finally took her into my arms and kissed her as if

tens of thousands of people weren't checking us out. Then we stopped kissing and started walking, and I told myself that in this stadium where I had been cheered by so many so often, I had just done something greater than any touchdown or Super Bowl victory: I had gotten back with the love of my life.

Flash Gortton joined us and the three of us just stood there for the longest time, too happy for words. We looked up and around, then at each other, and we burst out laughing.

I suppose we were laughing at all the poor souls who weren't Flash, Sheri or Red as we, our little family of three, clung to one another in that brisk, starry Canadian evening.